honeypot

Brenna Womer

Spuyten Duyvil

New York City

ISBN 978-1-949966-29-9

Cover art by Skyler Simpson

Library of Congress Cataloging-in-Publication Data

Names: Womer, Brenna, author.
Title: Honeypot / Brenna Womer.
Description: New York City : Spuyten Duyvil, [2019] | Includes selections of
    fiction and poetry.
Identifiers: LCCN 2019012648 | ISBN 9781949966299
Classification: LCC PS3623.O59743 A6 2019 | DDC 813/.6--dc23
LC record available at https://lccn.loc.gov/2019012648

We can mourn things / that weren't meant for us.

Diannely Antigua, *Ugly Music*

for Eve, Delilah, Jezebel, Bathsheba, and the Witch of Endor,
women cursed for their curiosity, sexuality, appetite, and intuition—

for the cautionary tales

CONTENTS

Fiction & Hybrid

    Nesting // 11

    The Cart or The Egg // 14

    IUD // 16

    Two Weeks, Guaranteed // 17

    Patsy Sings for Me // 19

    What's Mine is Yours // 26

    Anatomy of a Father, of a Moose // 27

Poetry

    All-Containered // 39

    When a Psychic Says We're Soul Mates // 40

    Language // 42

    tenure // 43

    slow burn // 44

    syncope // 45

    company // 46

    Paperweight // 48

    All the Trappings of // 49

    Back to My Place // 50

    birds of appetite // 51

    grandad // 53

    Tell me everything I know // 54

Creative Nonfiction

    Wüsthof Silverpoint II 10-Piece Set // 57

    Pet Euthanasia Consent // 59

    Motherlode // 61

    Male Doctors & My Anatomy // 63

    Forever Blonde // 65

    Cukes // 66

    Sate // 67

    Hypochondria, or The Disease // 72

    Empire Blue // 78

    -cosms 88

    We Are Not Saints // 89

Acknowledgements 97

Fiction & Hybrid

NESTING

Cayenne peppers are toxic to pigeons, but we didn't know. Marcie and I had just moved to Baltimore, both amiable, glass-half-full, small-town mid-Americans. We knew grouse and quail and duck; we knew songbirds. But the barrel-breasted, black-eyed pigeons who aimed their shit at car windshields and built flimsy nests on apartment ledges were a novelty, and not entirely unwelcome. Marcie liked the soft-gray rings around their eyes and the way their heads looked bald, she said, even though they were capped with feathers. People in the city called them sky rats and gutter birds, but Marcie took a shining to them the way she had with the barn mice and gophers back home. They were living, breathing, cooing reminders of life in rural Missouri, a state that southerners consider Midwestern but the North considers the South. Where exposed brick is not a stylistic choice, but, rather, indicative of a home that is *home* in the truest sense: well worn, neglected, and appreciated. Loved thin.

In her ad, our Baltimore landlord had used words like *modern* and *two-toned taupe*, but only uploaded a photo of the building's front, a brick façade of columns and pediment, deceptively regal and all too assuming. Exactly what Marcie and I expected of the city, and so we said we'd take the place. We didn't hate it.

Until I was 19, I spent summers on my grandparents' ranch, baling hay and mucking stalls. And Marcie grew up gardening alongside her mother. Surrounded by so many shades of city-gray, we thought to construct an aboveground pallet garden on the roof for herbs and tomatoes. We weren't sure what to fortify the garden against, so we asked the woman next door.

"Wind and squirrels," she said. "Stray cats and, of course, the pigeons."

We set a four-foot palisade of sharp, scrapped wood around the garden, with a little swing-door for prospective harvests. And when the time came, I'd sprinkle nascent fruit with cayenne pepper—a trick Marcie's mother used to dissuade the winged things. Every evening, home from work, we poured drinks, filled the green, plastic watering can, and climbed the back stairs to the roof. Sometimes, up there, we talked about our new jobs—hers in administration at Good Samaritan; mine, the reason we moved to the city, training linemen for Amtrak. But mostly, we talked about home, our families; mostly, we reminisced, or else enjoyed the silence, the amber rooftop light when the clouds broke. We'd yet to find much kindness in Baltimore.

On the evening we found our first produce budding in the garden, we were elated. I'd forgotten the pepper bag and had to run back downstairs for it while Marcie watered the supple, waxy bud, her eyes almost level with the soil. When she'd finished, I gave it a tender pinch of the pepper, which turned to a blood-red paste on contact with the wet leaves. We stood for a handful of minutes, the sun warm on our cheeks and collarbones, holding each other at the waist and sipping our cocktails.

Back downstairs in our apartment, infected with a grower's joy and a newfangled sense of something akin to belonging, we took turns mixing drink after stronger drink, dancing and flipping our favorite records from Side A to B and back again until one of us slipped fresh vinyl from its sleeve and pulled the needle. We slid across the hardwood floors on area rugs, and when Marcie pulled up her nightgown and bent herself over the back of the couch, we fucked without bothering to tilt the blinds.

The next morning when our alarms went off for work, we were sore, exhausted, and hung over, but Marcie kissed me good morning, still, with gummy lips and acid-foul breath. She showered first and made coffee and, while I was in the bathroom, popped her head in to say she was going to drink a cup on the roof, needed some fresh air and wanted to make sure she'd closed the garden gate.

A half-hour passed; I'd had breakfast and coffee and was dressed for work. But Marcie still hadn't come back down, and it wasn't like her to press herself for time. On my way out, I climbed the back stairs to the roof to say goodbye and found her sitting cross-legged in front of a dead pigeon. Her face was solemn, but I couldn't tell whether or not she'd been crying, and her mug was still full.

"We killed it," she said, and I walked over to look.

The pigeon was on its stomach with one wing open and its head resting against the pavement. Its eyes were a sickly red and swollen shut, and there was crusted foam beneath its beak. The first fruit was gone from the garden.

"The pepper didn't kill things at home. It just put them off," Marcie said, but without any affect or expression, I wasn't sure what was right or wrong to say.

"It's okay," I said, chancing a hand between her shoulder blades and moving my thumb in small circles. "We didn't know."

But she just stared at the pigeon.

After a few uncomfortable seconds, uncertain of whether to look at her or the bird, to stand up or move to sit, and knowing there were people a few miles away waiting on me to start their day, I asked Marcie if I should take the bird down to the dumpster on my way to the car. She shook her head no and picked up her mug, held out a hand for me to help her up.

"I've got it," she said, patting my chest but avoiding eye contact. "You should get to work."

*

At lunch that day in the break room, my boss gathered a few of us around his phone to watch a dash-cam video. He was a loud, enthusiastic man who seemed to require near-constant validation, a trait I was unaccustomed to in an overseer. On the screen were cars in traffic and a few utility poles.

"Wait for it," he said, and as a transformer blew, a row of pigeons fell like split-shot sinkers from the sky. Everyone laughed, and I obliged a smile. Someone asked him to replay and pause, so we could count the live pigeons on the line.

The Cart or the Egg

He was edging through the Sunday market crowd, smoking a cigarette like he'd done it once or twice before. His jeans were cuffed. There was a dog heeling at his side, content, but it wasn't his. Its nose cracked like dry clay. The man—Have I said his name?—was approached by a woman who was suddenly very close and stepping on the dog's paw, a green-gray patch of paste at her right shoulder from the ass of a parrot on a yarn leash.

The dog squawked and the bird snarled.

Hey, watch your step, that's a dog right there, the man said to the woman, who handed him a sweaty gum wrapper from between her soft, liver-spotted breasts. She left and the dog left too.

The note said, *Meet me two blocks south — ONE HOUR*, so he set a timer and sat down on the steps of a brownstone. He smoked the rest of his pack and when the timer chimed up, he walked again. She was there, two blocks south. The paste, crusted now, was still at her shoulder, but the bird was gone and she gripped the chipped handle of a shopping cart.

Guess how many, she said—Did I say the cart was filled with eggs?— but, not waiting for his guess, started a heave-shove-roll, one wheel twitching like a goat's lip.

I've got a good lead, she said. *Someone overturned at a checkpoint back on Chatham—a real mess—but I was ahead of the jam.*

Walking next to the cart, he had the urge to nudge the whole rig right over. It was the same kind of urge he'd had as a child during sermons, to stand up on a pew's strip of cushion, unzip his fly, and gyrate his hips so his genitals flapped in the direction of the baptismal pool. But he resisted as she pushed the first-place cart, while the second, steered by a boxy, Lego-looking man with his jaundiced tan, was suddenly not so far behind.

She said, *We'd better pitch it up a notch and make it count.*

They could see the finish. An old woman, gawped with lipstick, rotating her arm in a third-base-coach roundabout indicated they should sweep all the way through. Her arm like a ratchet, *cackt cackt cackt*, like one of those sprinkler heads, *acckt acckt acckt.* The Legoman's cart wheels were friction-hot-heat swiping at their heels.

I've got *these eggs*, she said, and gave the cart one rogue fever-heave. A dandelion pushed out of a crack by the table where the judges checked the eggs to see that they were not. Cracked.

He wouldn't ask her to share the prize because it would be like grocery shopping on a full stomach, which they say you should do but he thought not. He walked across the street, sat on the stoop of another brownstone—or maybe the stone was some other shade of business casual. He lit a cigarette and looked for the dog that wasn't his.

IUD

It was Halloweentime, and so the nurse had clipped a phosphorescent bug to her scrub-top pocket. It hung heavy over the tray of tools she was holding for the gynecologist, and I watched it slowly slip, unclip, and land beside the copper T. When the doctor had measured the inside of me, he said he thought my sacred space was too small, unaccommodating, though I did meet the minimum requirement set by the manufacturer.

Would you like to proceed, he asked.

The beetle was there on the tray—

Go on, I said.

—next to molded copper.

The doctor took up his pincers, curved and studded to grip like Dungeness cracked at my annual birthday lunch. (Twenty-four and wearing a bib that said, *ITS MY BIRTHDAY AND ALL I GOT WAS CRABS.*)

The nurse didn't notice the doctor grab the bug from the tray; the doctor didn't notice the beetle in his claw as he reached into the dark, its transition from milky green to neon—a childish magic I believed in till the day I learned. He leaned up from between my legs, smacked the glove from his right hand, and said, *Success!* But for days after I could feel it moving, pipe-cleaner antennae feeling for the thresholds of fallopian tubes, and, finding their way, bottlebrush pain as they pushed into the wet and soft of me. The elytra worked to open, and I could feel their pressure at my walls; tarsi scraped and mandible clipped at endometrium. I went in for an emergency checkup, told them something wasn't right.

The pain, I said, sweat-soaked, and the same nurse took me in for an ultrasound, with nothing attached, now, to her scrub top pocket.

She wobbled the wand through cold gel at my lower abdomen and stopped over the implant. Soothed by megahertz, the thing lay still and haloed, phosphorescence in black and white, but no movement, and no pain.

Looks fine to me, hon, the nurse said. *Everything's right where it should be. How's your pain?*

Better, I said, but all I could see was the glow of sawtooth feelers and tips of creeping paper wings.

Two Weeks, Guaranteed

I pick up a chunk of turquoise from a velvet-lined case, smooth a thumb over its surface and think of Dickinson chiding her honest fingers after a noonday nap under the pines, under an oak, under the Bodhi Tree like Siddhartha. A Navajo man with aged-blue tattoos is dressed like my father in a plaid button-up, in cargo jeans, and says, "Turquoise is the protector stone. It was tradition for warriors to wear it on hunts and into battle. But it is not an excuse to be reckless. It only protects up to 50 miles per hour."

Stuck in traffic next to an aqua-blue, '61 Chevy Biscayne, two boys in the back—brothers, no more than a year or two apart. No seatbelts, maybe lap belts, and Dad in the driver seat. His hair is greasy, long and blonde. His left hand grips the steering wheel at 12 o'clock, right arm stretched along the back of the bench seat, empty. Mom at home making deviled eggs; Mom laid up in bed with another migraine; Mom long gone. They're out for a Saturday drive, picking two books each at the library for smarts, looking for four-leafs in the clover field for luck, digging arrowheads at the quarry for courage.

The woman whispers to herself as she trims my cuticles, but the whisper is not meant to be a whisper, is heard by the man in a surgical mask sanding acrylics two stations down. The woman does not look at me while she massages my forearms with lavender lotion; she keeps her eyes trained on the television, the close-captioned rerun of *Walker, Texas Ranger*. She does not look at me when she takes away my credit card or brings it back with a receipt, does not look me in the eye until I tell her I like her bracelet.

"Jade?" I ask.

"Yes," she says, and smiles.

But the bracelet is so small, barely wider than her wrist, a solid circle with no clasp. She could never take it off, not with shampoo or butter or baby oil. I ask where she got it.

"My mother gave it to me when I was eight years old," she says.

And I understand she grew into the bracelet. To age a tree, you have to cut it open and count the rings. To remove the bracelet, she would have to cut through her arm or cut through the bracelet.

"Do you want shellac?" she asks. "It'll last two weeks, guaranteed."

Patsy Sings for Me

Turns out I'm pregnant. I suppose I have to tell Dale now that I'm certain. Chances are this wasn't what he thought he was getting himself into that night he put Patsy on the jukebox at Flynn's Tavern and asked me if I'd like to dance real slow—sticky-hot beer breath on my cheek, his scratchy flannel thick with cigarette smoke. I've tried smoking, but I'm just no good at it. I like that he does, though. I know I'm supposed to scold him, tell him the things will kill him if he doesn't quit, but I love how they make him smell and he just looks so good with a pointer curled around the filter. Maybe that makes me a bad person. Selfish. But I don't have much time left being selfish, so I'm just going to enjoy his smell a little while longer.

*

This funny guy came into the diner by himself just now and sat in my section, in one of my booths. I hate it when people ignore the sign. It says right there, "Please reserve booths for two or more guests," so I asked him, "Sir, do you have another one coming or is it just you to-night," and he looked at me all confused and stuttered, saying he wasn't sure, there might be someone, but he didn't know if she'd show up or not. He seemed antsy, nervous. We aren't too busy tonight, so I figure he can sit in my booth until we are. At shift change, Charity gave me one of those motherhood magazines. I can't believe how much they charge for baby shoes.

That girl showed up. The guy in my booth spilled his coffee all over his book when she walked in. It's been three hours, and they're still here. They've killed an entire pot between the two of them, and they're on their second round of ham and waffles. I don't think I've ever seen two people laugh so much together. Dale and I don't really laugh like that. Sometimes we laugh at the same jokes on TV. He laughs when I ask him if he'd still love me if I got fat, laughs and says, "Your titties'd get bigger, and I'd love that."

My titties haven't gotten any bigger yet.

I told Dale last night. He didn't have much to say, but Dale never really has much to say. I thought he was maybe happy for a minute, because for him happy starts out the same way as mad. He takes off his ball cap and rubs the back of his neck, but if he's happy he puts the cap back on and smiles. Last night he threw it across the room. He didn't make a fuss but left pretty quick. I watched his truck peel out of the driveway and knew he wasn't off to buy a baby-name book.

The funny guy and that girl are here again, same day as last week, but they came together this time. We have this jukebox that's four songs for a dollar, and they're doing this thing where he puts in a dollar and picks a song and sits down and then she gets up, picks a song, and sits down. They do this with each dollar then talk and laugh until the songs run out, and then he gets up and puts another dollar in and they do it again.

The two of them don't acknowledge anyone in the place except me to take their order. They're real polite, though. Smile a lot. They play these old songs, ones my parents used to listen to. I suppose they're about my age—twenty-two, twenty-three maybe—but I feel years older than them. I can't help thinking that maybe it's because they're having fun. That night at Flynn's after we were done dancing, Dale pinched my arm and pulled me in real close, asked if I wanted to go have a little fun.

I'm not sure why Dale decided to stick around after I told him about the baby. Not that he's a bad guy—he's not. He just isn't the stick-around type. I didn't hear from him for a month after we hooked up, then he showed up at my door one morning asking if I'd missed him. A few days later I found out about the baby.

I wonder how things would be different if Dale and I were like Funny Guy and That Girl. What if Dale had been all nervous when I walked into Flynn's, had stuttered when he asked me to dance? What if we played each other love songs at 2 AM on the jukebox at some nowhere truck-stop diner? What if he knew how to make me laugh? But I'm not That Girl. I'm the one who gets knocked up in the cab of a truck and driven home by some still-drunk drifter who passes out on her couch.

*

Dale took off again. I'm not sure where he went, but he scribbled "3 days" on some receipt paper and pinned it to the fridge. Charity says I shouldn't hold my breath, says I should go ahead and make an appointment at the clinic. "The earlier the better," she says.

*

Today's the third day and Dale hasn't even called. That damn couple's here again, putting love songs on the jukebox and acting like they're not playing them for each other. Like they're just in the mood to hear "You Make My Dreams Come True" or "Sugar Pie, Honey Bunch." Makes me want to spit on their waffles before spraying the whipped cream.

*

Dale called last night on a pay phone from God knows where. He was drunk, and I couldn't understand much of what he said. When there was a quiet moment I told him I was thinking about having a doctor take care of things before I got too far along. He started crying heavy sobs like only a man lets loose when his mother dies or he finds Jesus. And then he hung up the phone.

*

Funny Guy's here, the usual booth and time, but it's been about an hour and That Girl hasn't shown up. He keeps looking out the window, and he's not being rude to me or anything, but he's not smiling either. He seemed different when he came in. Heavy. He only ordered coffee and put on Patsy's "Crazy." I think he and I both got a little lost in it. It's been over a week and Dale's not back yet. I'd been keeping his "3 days" note in my apron pocket, but tonight I finally threw it away. Then I ate the ham and waffles Funny Guy didn't order.

Charity told me she got pregnant when she was sixteen and went to the clinic, said I could ask her questions if I wanted. I asked about the appointment, how it felt before and after and if she was scared and if the doctor was nice to her. She said it wasn't as painful or dramatic as she expected. That it felt like bad cramps and pressure in spots you wouldn't expect, and she said she cried a little bit but wasn't even sure why. No one went with her, but she lied and said she had someone to pick her up and then just drove herself home and watched movies the rest of the day. She didn't even have to give up her shift the next morning.

Funny Guy and That Girl are both here, same time, same booth, but they came separately and they're not putting anything on the jukebox. He's watching her face so carefully, but she won't hold eye contact with him for very long. She keeps shaking her head and looking down at the paper placemat. He'll ask a question, all calm and sad-looking, and she'll just shake her head again. They started talking like this before I could get over there to take their food order, but I doubt either of them has much of an appetite. Heartache does that. So does growing a baby in your gut. Between the two I haven't been able to keep much down. I don't think Dale's coming back.

That Girl left first, then Funny Guy came up to the register and apologized for not ordering anything. I told him it was okay and that I've been real tired lately and didn't mind the down time. He just stood at the register for a second not saying anything but looking like he wanted to say something. I started to feel the silence and told him the place was real quiet without them playing the jukebox. I think that was the wrong thing to say because his eyes started getting glossy. I panicked and said something about how they seemed like a sweet couple and that I could tell something was different tonight and I'm sorry and hope everything turns out okay.

He stuffed his hands in his pockets and said, "Thanks. You probably won't be seeing us here together again, but if she ever comes in with someone else, maybe play some Patsy for me, okay?"

I told him I'd do that and not to worry about the coffee tab. After he walked out I unplugged the jukebox for the night.

*

When the pregnancy test read positive, I bought this notebook because I thought it might be good for me to write things down, to remember how it all happened and what pregnancy was like and what all was going on while he or she was inside of me. But now it just feels like I've been writing down all the sad and bad and lonely in my life and other people's.

I made an appointment a week from today. Same place Charity went. Maybe I won't have to miss a shift either.

*

Tomorrow's the day. I noticed my stomach pooching out this morning and my boobs finally started to swell a little. Without Dale here to notice or care, though, it's really just a pain in the ass because none of my bras fit.

That Girl is here tonight, same booth—same side of the booth even—same time. I went to refill her coffee and didn't see she was crying until it was too late and I was already reaching for her cup. I asked her if she was all right, and she said she was sorry and she hadn't seen the sign until just then. She pointed to "Please reserve booths for two or more guests," and I told her it was fine, that I didn't mind and she could stay as long as she wanted. She nodded and walked over to the jukebox. She put on Patsy's "Stand By Your Man." What are the odds of that? She sat down and didn't make a scene but kept crying. I had the thought that these kids—just a whisper older or younger than me—they don't know what Patsy's singing about. Funny Guy doesn't know my kind of loneliness, and That Girl wouldn't know how to stand by her man through the thick and thin of it. How to stand by him even when he's cold and hard and gone.

I'm the girl who gets knocked up in the cab of a truck, but I'm also the girl who makes bacon and eggs in the morning if he's still around when I wake up. I'm the girl who gets receipt paper scrawled with a lie and keeps it in her pocket, pulling it out on breaks to remind herself that he cared enough to leave a note. I'm the girl who gets a drunken phone call at four in the morning after an eight-hour overnight at a shithole diner and listens to him cry and ramble and still tells him to come home, wherever he is, come back to me.

Tonight, she put on Patsy, but last week when Funny Guy—the one who pays a quarter a song for four hours straight; the one who orders two rounds of breakfast and bottomless coffees and won't let her touch the check; the Funny Guy who takes it as a challenge when she stops laughing for more than a minute's time—when he was staring out the window just a foot from where she's sitting right now, hoping she'd show up, where was she? What did she think she had found that was so much better? There is nothing better. She doesn't know what it means to stand by her man, but I'll bite my tongue let her think she's the one Patsy's singing for.

*

After that last shift I only had a few hours to sleep before my appointment, and I got home to find Dale on my porch. He was sober and asked if I'd missed him. He asked if he was too late. I sat on the couch and he crouched at my feet and held onto my ankles, saying, "Please, I love you. I need you, please." He made all these promises about staying put and providing, and he cried without me trying to make him. I told him I loved him too, but that I'd had the procedure done days ago. I said I was so tired from work, but he could stay on the couch, and we'd talk after I got some rest. A couple hours later my alarm went off for me to get up and dressed for the clinic. I went downstairs and found fifty dollars on the dinette with a note that said, "My share."

*

Boss lets me keep a stool behind the register now, which makes writing a whole lot easier. I hunch less and don't have to shift my weight from foot to foot. It's their night but the booth is empty, and I've got the jukebox playing songs somewhere between happy and sad. Last night I made myself spaghetti and when I went to throw away the empty sauce jar I had this idea. I cut a slit in the metal lid, big enough for tips and change, and made a label for the outside. I figure I should start saving now because baby shoes don't come cheap.

What's Mine is Yours

The time she was tanning in the backyard, her skin bronze against the neon plastic of the foldout chair. It was late afternoon, and I was in my velcroed sandals, angry because the mower wouldn't start. A yank too hard and too fast on the pull cord burned my hand, and I stood screaming in the calf-high grass. A scream, she said, that stuck hot to her skin like wet tar, the neighbors watching from their aboveground pool.

You'd think I would remember who bought the pillowcases and the shower curtain and the dish soap, but I don't. And I don't want them, but I can't just leave them if they're mine, and I don't want to take anything at all because I want to fix things, but she doesn't want to fix things, and I can't make her. So I take the pillowcases and leave the shower curtain and say fuck the dish soap.

At the end I said, *I'll do whatever it takes.*

And at the end she said, *It's too late for that now.*

It was her idea to move in together. I thought it was too soon but said okay because she was the one paying for an apartment she never slept at. But the moving in was good. Mail came with both of our names on it. She cooked, and I cleaned; gin in the freezer for her, and whiskey in the cupboard for me. And every night we sat on the cement porch steps and watched people pass, holding hands, and walking dogs, and waving, or not, and it felt like things might be good forever.

When I couldn't mow the lawn and the backyard started losing light, she made enchiladas for dinner. I pulled them from the oven and dropped the pan, *motherFUCKER,* and the sauce burned our feet. She got a towel. We cleaned the kitchen floor together and then shared a bowl of Easy Mac with too much pepper, and after we were done she said, *Fill the bowl with water so the cheese won't stick.* That night when the sky was dark and the neighbors' house was quiet, I watched her walk alone through our shaggy grass to their pool, climbed the ladder to soak her feet.

Anatomy of a Father, of a Moose

Dad didn't like guns. He was a military man and a decent shot, but he didn't like their weight, their potential. He preferred the hollow ones attached by a tube to the front of *Area 51* in the base arcade where we killed aliens and shot off screen to reload. During his two deployments in Bosnia, my ages seven and nine, he had to sling an M16 across his back every morning before he left the barracks. He deployed to Iraq when I was thirteen and Kuwait when I was fourteen, and during that time he holstered a 9mm at his right thigh. He never had to shoot, though. Never even reached for the guns. His job kept him behind a desk and away from any combat, but he had to carry one anyway, part of the uniform. Dad was a quiet man, strong and honest—gentle, and I loved him for it. We didn't know each other well, which is odd to say about a father who wasn't absent in the usual sense. He provided, never willingly abandoned, but was absent nevertheless.

When he got back from Kuwait I was fifteen and we received orders to an airbase in the heart of Alaska. It was a two-week road trip from the Virginia coast, just the three of us. I watched movies in the back seat, picking new ones at Wal-Marts in every state we crossed or clipped—each of us in our own little worlds. Mom wasn't a mystery to me, and I didn't wonder what she thought about or have questions tucked away I was too nervous to ask. It was a mutual discomfort between Dad and me, father and daughter. We were both at a loss and Mom was there floating between us.

When we arrived at our new home in August, the first snow of the season had yet to fall, but the days were cool and the nights already cold. The nearest town was North Pole, which was home to The Santa Clause House (open year-round), a Blockbuster, a McDonalds, and a grocery store open from eight to eight. We attended Pioneer Baptist—a small, wooden church painted white and carved into a grove of birches. At a glance it looked like a one-room, but it was two stories with the Sunday school rooms on the first floor and the sanctuary in the basement. The foyer was carpeted, and during the eight months there was snow on the ground and for breakup in spring the carpet was a sponge you couldn't ring out, one big mudroom. Downstairs the floors were tiled in white vinyl and there was a kitchen at the back with an industrial Bunn coffee maker from the eighties. Every Sunday there was a morning service, a potluck lunch, and an afternoon service so no one had to brave the roads to come back in the evening.

The first time I tried moose was in a potluck chili Pastor Jack's wife, Linda, brought for lunch one Sunday in late September. It was good chili, and I never would have known except she asked me how I liked the moose meat. We were still new to the area, and I'm sure she guessed I'd never had it. She said it was the last from the church hunt the year before.

"The men go every October, take the older boys and do some father-son bonding," she said. "We'll have to see if we can't get your dad to come along this year."

Mom was home sick that Sunday, so Dad let me drive home after second service. I navigated the sheets of ice with caution in our white Ford Expedition, the one we'd driven across the States and up through Canada.

"Miss Linda said all the church men go on a moose hunt next month," I said to Dad, who was in the passenger seat. "She said they're gonna try and get you to go."

"Yeah, Jack invited me last week. I was thinking about it."

"But you don't hunt," I said, turning my head to look at him. A warm sensation gripped the nape of my neck at the thought of him coming home with blood on his boots, on his gloves. "You don't even own a gun."

"Eyes on the road," he said, pointing us into the white ahead. "It's what they do here, and Jack said I could use one of his. They're just trying to keep the population down in the woods near town. Moose cause a lot of accidents." He considered this a moment, and then said—more to himself, it seemed, than to me—"It's actually more of a moral obligation."

Back at the house, Mom had soup on the stove—bouillabaisse in the Dutch oven her mother let her take when she left home. Its red enamel coating had chipped some from the lid and the handles, and the white inside was stained and burned from decades of roasts and curries and

28

sauces. Dad kissed Mom on the cheek and went into the living room to watch football, and I hopped onto the counter next to a sticky cutting board that was pungent with garlic and onion. Mom drank from a bottle of chardonnay before measuring a cup for the pot and then added a pinch each of fennel, celery seed, and saffron.

"I think Dad's going on a hunting trip with the men from church," I said, ripping at an onion skin.

"Oh, I doubt that." She slid her finger down the list of ingredients to find her place. "You know he doesn't care for guns."

"He said he was thinking about it. I don't like it. I'm not sure why, but I just don't. Miss Linda said it's some father-son thing, too."

"Well, I'll be surprised if he goes, but if he does, he knows what he's doing. Are you afraid he'll get hurt?"

"No." I ran a hand through my hair before realizing it smelled like onion. "I don't know. What if he likes it?"

"Would that be so bad? He's never really had a hobby, just sports," she said. I could hear the referee's call echoing in the other room. "Neither of us has many friends here yet. It could be good for him."

"It doesn't freak you out, the idea of him killing something?"

She stopped stirring and thought before answering.

"I guess I'm not crazy about the idea, but I wouldn't say it freaks me out. I trust your father. He's a good man, hon, he really is. I know you don't feel very close to him right now." She set the spoon down, turning to me. "You know what? You should go with him."

"What?" I asked, glancing at his flattop bristling above the back of the lounger. "I can't go *hunting*. Besides, it's a guys' trip anyway. He probably wouldn't even want me to go."

"Well, you never know until you ask," she said, taking up the spoon again.

The soup was boiling.

Dad and I hadn't talked much since he came back from Kuwait. Really, we hadn't talked much since I got that stomach ache in Barnes & Noble when I was eleven and then wiped red in the bathroom stall. I could remember a time when he was my favorite person, a time when my problems were easy to solve. A scraped knee asked a few splashes of peroxide and a Popsicle to ease the pain, and a ride on his shoulders let me see high above the crowd at the Fourth of July air show on the flight line behind our house.

When I was thirteen and my first boyfriend broke up with me, Mom sat on my daybed and let me cry into her lap, Dad downstairs in the living room. She stroked my hair, and I wiped at the snot bubbling from my nose with the sleeve of my hoodie. After about twenty minutes, I heard him walking up the stairs and thought he might be coming to hold a few of my broken pieces, to teach me something about boys and the ways of love and call me sweetheart. He pushed the door open but didn't come in, only stood there and asked, his voice gentle and a touch higher than its usual pitch, if I wouldn't like to come downstairs and play a few hands of Gin Rummy.

The Sunday before the hunt, Pastor Jack brought Dad a .270 Winchester. During potluck, when the boys usually pulled parkas and boots over their Sunday best to chase each other through the woods, instead they all gathered around Pastor's tailgate as he handed the rifle over to Dad. He pointed out its various features, telling him to smooth his hand over the walnut stock, selling him on the hunt less than a week away. I sipped lukewarm Folgers and watched from a window in the foyer, the carpet squishing under my feet. I hadn't asked if I could go with him, still wasn't sure I wanted to. I watched him with the rifle, turning it over in his hands, pulling at knobs and levers, glancing through the scope. He handled it so naturally, there with snow clumped in the tread of his boots. My father who didn't like guns for reasons he never gave, but maybe it was because he knew what bad men were capable of, how much they could take without asking. Maybe he thought it was something in the blood.

Dad's father was an Army man and a drunk. I learned this from my mother, as I did most things I know about my father's life, at the kitchen counter after she'd poured her second drink. His father received a Bad Conduct Discharge when Dad was thirteen. This was the grandfather I never met, who died of lung cancer when I was a baby. Dad spent his teenage years up late making sure his father made it to the couch, but keeping him out of his sisters' room and away from his mother, who had taken to washing down her sleeping pills with gin. There was a time, Mom said, that he sat at the top of the stairs and watched his father work the doorknob under the back porch light, watched his hazy form through the window; he'd learned it was best not to try and speed things along. He heard the key ting against the ground and then saw his father's fist come through the bottom pane of glass, reaching around for the twist lock, blood on the white gossamer curtain. It chewed up his hand and wrist pretty well, nicked an artery; Dad wrapped his father's hand in a dishtowel before driving to the urgent care. On her third glass of wine she added to the story that sometimes Dad said he wished he'd just gone to bed and let his father bleed out on the kitchen floor.

My breath fogged the glass as a little boy tugged at Dad's coat as he considered the rifle. Dad smiled down at the boy as a father would a son, with a different kind of love in his eyes. He held the gun out for the boy to run his little hand across. He would have liked to have had a son, would have been better with a boy than he was with me; Mom has said so too. Dad nodded to Pastor and then walked to put the gun in our trunk. They shook hands and came back in together, past me at the window.

"Young lady, we're turning your father into a true Alaska woodsman," he said, patting my back and spilling my coffee. Dad smiled at the thought.

At home, he unloaded the gun from the trunk, and I clapped my boots in the mudroom. When he came through the door, I asked without thinking, with just a picture of the little boy from church in my head, "Can go on that hunting trip with you?"

He was quiet, which wasn't unusual, and hung up his coat.

"I know it's a guys' trip and more of a father-son thing, but you said it's what they do here and I could probably learn something, you know?" I said, nervous, rambling. "I don't really want to shoot anything, and I know you have to have a license for that anyway, but I'd like to come along and watch. I could help carry things. I promise I won't talk this much."

"Well, I think that'd be fine," he said, and laughed.

"Yeah?" I smiled because I couldn't help it. "You don't think anyone'll mind?"

"I guess we're kind of bucking tradition." He paused. "But I'll talk to Jack. If they're all bringing their sons and you want to come along I don't see why it'd be problem." He brushed at the back of his neck. "We'll butcher the moose afterward, though, back at the church. I guess you could help the ladies back in the kitchen with lunch?"

"I think I'd be okay, maybe," I said, trying not to think of wet fur and serrated knives, of dead eyes and dry tongues. "But I can come?"

"You can come. We leave 7am Saturday."

I can remember only one story from Dad's childhood that he told me himself. It was a hot day during summer vacation and he was nine. He and his brother were biking home from the pool, and they stopped by the air-conditioned bank where they knew the tellers put donuts out for customers in the afternoon. They leaned their bikes against the bushes and peeked through the glass as they strategized, locating the platter on a lobby table and then walking quietly through the doors when the tellers were occupied. They grabbed two each from the table and ran out, stuffed the donuts in their mouths and took off on their bikes. They stopped a couple blocks away to enjoy them properly.

This was the story Dad told. When I asked him for another, a family trip or his first date or what he was like in school, he said he had a bad memory, couldn't remember much else. My guess is there were many nights of drunken accidents and broken glass; nights spent herding his parents to soft places they could sleep off their respective stupors. My guess is he remembered plenty more than chocolate donuts on a hot afternoon, just nothing he wanted to burden me with at ages eight or ten or twelve. Eventually I stopped asking.

The morning of the hunt I layered long underwear under sweatpants under snow pants and stuffed the pockets of my coat with extra hand warmers. We had neck gaiters and thick caps and gloves so stiff with insulation I could barely move my fingers. Mom filled a green Stanley thermos with hot black coffee and wrapped up two toasted Pop-Tarts for me. We rode with Pastor Jack and his son and one of the deacon's boys who snorted when he saw the pink frosting and sprinkles in my paper towel. The boys were a little older than me—seventeen or so. They talked locations, guns and bullets. Dad and I were quiet, new to the game, and so it seemed, for at least a moment, two points on the same line. I sipped coffee from the thermos lid and passed it to Dad, who took it with a small smile and a nod. I looked out the window, at a place still so new to me. The early-morning Alaska cold was like a pause, like something that was already a memory.

When we got out of the car I shouldered the bag closest to me, and Dad took up the Winchester. As men piled out of other trucks and loaded guns I watched the fluid surrender of civil twilight to sunrise. We set out on the hunt and I kept stride with my father, the swish of our snow pants falling in and out of rhythm. As we walked, I thought of blood pooled in clear plastic stretched across the white tile floor where Pastor Jack gave his sermons and read verses from a worn leather copy of the King James. I thought of the red satin sash draped over the wooden cross behind the pulpit. I thought of the grandfather I never met and how his blood was Dad's blood and that blood was mine. I thought of the gun strapped to his back, holstered at his thigh, the one he held now with two hands, the one he'd use for killing, that would make it easier to kill.

It was an hour before he took a shot. The other men had scattered with their boys, and it was just the two of us in a clearing. When he set himself and took aim for the bull's lung cavity, I paused with the cold and breathed heavy against wet fleece. I'm not sure why, I still don't know why, but he flinched. The bullet missed the torso entirely, hitting instead the bull's jaw. From Dad's mouth came a white cloud, a piercing, anguished cry louder than the crack of the bullet, the crack of the moose's jaw, and he took off after the thing which had run back into the trees. I tried to keep up, but with the boots and layers and a bag bouncing at my hip, I didn't make it far. I stopped, out of breath, with the red trail at my feet; the moose would bleed out, or starve to death if it didn't. Dad had disappeared, and with none of the other men in sight, I waited. I dropped the bag at my feet and took two hand warmers from my pocket. I peeled open the foil and slipped the white packets into the palms of my gloves. Another shot cut through the silence. It felt so much colder standing still and time seemed to stop with me. There was no wind, no movement in the trees or on the ground. The snow was bright, blinding, but I couldn't see the sun, no blue in the sky. I'm not sure how long I had been waiting when I saw Dad emerge from the tree line; it could have been two minutes or twenty. I walked to meet him. His mouth was exposed, and when we were close I saw his eyes were red and wet.

"Did you find it?" I asked, pulling my mask down too.

Our breath met between us in a puff of white and I saw little icicles had formed over the hairs of his mustache.

"Yes," he said. "Put your mask back on. I need to find Jack."

Some of the men congregated, and Pastor sent the boys and me into the surrounding woods for sturdy branches to prop open the ribcage. I wanted to do right by my father, for us to experience something new and hard and good together, to be reminded of the blood we shared. And though I didn't know if this—the killing and butchering—was the right thing, I knew it was a start. When the boys and I got back, the men were already at work. Pastor had cut the moose from stern to stem and asked Dad to stand on one side of the body; they curled their fingers inside and counted to three. I stood with my back against a tree, staring up at the white Alaskan light, a mess of treetops. There was a pop, and the boys were ready with the branches. They wedged a couple inside, and Pastor began hefting out what was never meant to be seen by anyone but God. Dad reached his hands in too, and as he removed a weighty, steaming organ—I wasn't sure which one—with such care, I was surprised at the intimacy. The red mass overflowed from his two palms and strained at the gaps between his fingers. He placed it on the plastic they'd laid out, and I took a few steps toward him.

"Can I?" I asked, gesturing to the cavity.

Dad looked to Pastor. "Mind if she helps me with the heart?"

I put on gloves and reached in with him; we cupped our hands around the thick muscle, and once we began to lift I knew he could have done it alone. I thought that from the inside, death would be more obvious, like the slick stillborn I'd seen delivered in a movie, clearly cold and gone, but the moose's heart was still hot and so red you'd have expected it to beat. We set it next to the other parts, and Pastor kept on until the moose was empty. When it was time to skin it, he made the cuts, peeled back a lip of fur, and asked me if I'd like to take a side. I looked to Dad, who gave me a nod and what I think was the beginning of a smile he decided was not appropriate given the circumstances. Pastor counted down again from three, and we jerked at the skin together until it separated from the white membrane coating the bones and muscle, like the thin layer beneath the shell of a hard-boiled egg.

"Not bad, young lady," he said to me. "Your dad and I've got it from here."

"How about you see if there's any of that coffee left," Dad said before taking up the saw.

Dad and I drove home in silence with a trunk full of wrapped meat, parcels they'd divvied up back at the church where Miss Linda and some of the wives had been waiting with pans of noodles masked by congealed layers of cheese. When we pulled into the driveway he put the car in park and turned to me.

"Do you think we could keep the hunt between us?" He looked earnest and a little afraid, though I wasn't sure what there was to be afraid of. "I didn't mean to yell like that or to leave you behind when I went to chase down the moose, and, if it's all the same to you, I'd prefer your mother didn't know."

"I won't say anything," I said; then added, "and I wasn't scared. Of you, or anything else."

"Good, sweetheart." He popped the trunk, and we carried the meat, piece by piece, to the deep freeze.

POETRY

ALL-CONTAINERED

Smoke apart the closed
and fire the remains;
add pears, something
green, to the kitchen.

Own up to the life locked
in the washroom; white,
but for soot-black froth
from lip to gummy lip,
and blue feet.

Use a word that crunches
like a sun-bleached egg
in the mouth and throat
because you didn't ask for
a *miracle* but got one
anyway, would prefer
a life of quiet good
and discomfort to these
grand gestures and tragic
oversights of the Universe.

Understand you can be
nothing or everything to
this world, that there is
no in-between, and that
to be nothing is not to
have or do nothing, but
to live and die in wet
cement. And to be every-
thing is not to have and
do everything, but to
watch all the nothing
in slow motion from
the grass.

WHEN A PSYCHIC SAYS WE'RE SOUL MATES

You expect room,
space
beyond pines;
Kings of Up, Sideways.
For a good time, die, forever.
Bible tells me bodies hurt,
perfect beasts—wild, dark,
promised.

Years of silver, play china.
This is the runaway; the last,
smashed, alone I love you.
This waltz in the woods (the
stone, the show, dumb sky,
paranormal sunshine). A little
galaxy, misery; hills spark
green. Few men take this walk,
this war. Night rises and the
whale, dog, spider, frail cock:
things I hate.

Spy our keepers; the last days,
nights. Rise, Brother! Magic
child, seeking. End the days
now, white heart (magnolia—)
my best shame.
You horrible paradise:
lost, lost, lost.

We talk about love, the retreat,
and who lives, hearts blue, and
cigarettes, and the girl in the
realms of dilemma, running
clueless with grizzly hours,
getting fat.

Recall how you know the heart,
and remember the future, the
brain, the chronic hunger and
burn; life in a wet summer, loud
and close—eternal, intolerable.

Number the young.

LANGUAGE

I wanted
him to fuck me

until he said
he wanted to,

until he forced it
into syllables

I can count
on one hand.

TENURE

I trade my body for good company   or company   more often than
not   but professor doesn't see me in the hallway   copy room
elevator   parking lot doesn't see me
    if my tit's not in his mouth   when his red stag isn't dribble
down my chin   and sticky   to the leather of his couch like
my grandparents' couch   the family I don't call family because
they only love me during second service   vacation bible school
bless this food and the *women* who prepared it   a family by any
other name   is a sexual history
    an untethered novelty   so I ask him about his parents but
of course   they're dead of course   because professor is so
many years of being   a white man in this world   in this
grad-student pussy   is sixty-five years of asking   *let's go to
the bedroom*
    and I am forty fewer of   *okay*

SLOW BURN

my age always closer to the scotch in his glass
we slow-dance
next to the pool table
he asks me *follow* but I
can't didn't don't
know how and his arms are rigid and his hand
too firm at my waist his fingers
like a trowel in my stubborn soil but he keeps
his eyes closed because it doesn't need to be me
"me and mrs jones" and my uncooperative   body   always
taking up more space than it should
        he asks again *just follow damnit*   but I'm drunk on light
beer and can't make any more or less of myself   and I know
he has a wife at home   that they sleep in separate beds and
her name is Gretchen   but I'm in a sundress and a fresh
twenty-one while his cheek is   whisker-burn against my own
like my father's when he used to kiss me
goodnight

SYNCOPE

I shit blood for three days after
did you know that
from the room
feel
without being broken
a life-raft inflates
the brain
the shower curtain
my own body
him and his
and splotches of black dead
and back to bed
such a shame
again

he slipped and missed and
a woman will excuse herself
so you can't watch her
so she can be hurt
by a pain so acute that
to insulate
grab hold of
the fear of touching
of being touched by
cock-hard inattention
hot and numb
where he asks
I was about to come

COMPANY

put on a show
for me
he asks
while I ride
on top
and wonder
what it is
he thinks
I'm doing
now
does he
think I mash
my own breasts
and pinch
nipples hard
and red and
raw at home
alone
with my dogs
watching
he asks
tell me what
you really want
tell me where
you want it
but I want
to go back
to the couch
and eat
my cold
bagel but
I know he
has to
come before

I get
my everything
toasted
with plain
cream cheese

PAPERWEIGHT

Weed smoked gone from rolling paper
down to roach paperclip.
He paperbound her wrists,
pushed inside, paper-sack deep.

Months and no wallpaper peeled and shed,
no toilet paper red, so she went
to the clinic.
Lobby waits with *Marie Claire,*
The View on mute;
not-today's newspaper print.
She should've come sooner.
Leaned back on a fresh stretch of tissue paper,
a mobile overhead like a crib—
paper crane, paper tiger, paper plane.

The doctor asked *okay*, then paper cut.
Paperweight on paper plate;
she held the nurse's hand.
In the recovery room, no vinegar
or brown paper bag, but a cookie
for the sugar in her glass-paper blood.
A friend drove her home to thick pads
papered over Hanes Her Way.

ALL THE TRAPPINGS OF

In the days after nights I dream of you, three years feels nearer than a hangnail, than a raspberry seed in the teeth,

because you've ruined me with your ripe red nipples, your sad blue eyes; and how am I still so small with a thousand ugly miles between our ungroomed bodies?

I would die with my mouth wedged open, with peanut butter on my tongue, if it meant you'd walk me to the tree line just to drop me at your feet—

BACK TO MY PLACE

I can't remember
if we kissed;
The night to me is squares
of black and blankets.
"Don't. I haven't shaved
in months."
I can't remember
his hands,
how they moved, but
in the morning
a condom in the trashcan,
Full
of white, and he is gone.
The door unlocked and the lights on
in my dead Christmas tree.

BIRDS OF APPETITE

miso honey & vinegar
in a slender silver spoon;
oregano flower, pickled
peach, smoked salmon
and cantaloupe: *taste*—
taste, taste. because honey
isn't sweet until the
vinegar is bitter;

until you are onions and
cigarettes while we fuck
in a broken office chair;

until I say *i love you* with
a tongue thick as dried
apricot and you say it
back and kiss me with hot
teeth and sesame breath;

until I love you more than
I hate you, and we're high
more often than not;

until you can't roll the pasta
any thinner and the meringue
is whipped to sog and neither
of us knows why it hurts as
much to be loved as it does
to be forgotten;

until the cake we make
together is soft and salt
and butter-clean and you
proffer a crust of it to my
impatient mouth, watering
for the slick glove of your
eager, practiced hand.

GRANDAD

twists handkerchiefs into mice   makes them jump from his palm with a flick of fingers under
the tail, his nails   thick and yellow, just on the one hand   like mustard he can't scrub off
          dirty old man, mom says of my father's father   porn in the folds of his recliner
an ashtray in every room

grandad walks me for a 99 flake   shows me how to make the dry maple seeds helicopters
his hair is greasy, white
corn silk   and his little blue eyes drip karo when I laugh   he is not yet a decade sober

grandad talks aa and john wayne   keeps butterscotch candies in his pocket
          wrings his hands like a landed fly   he's proud
of the chocolate cake he makes with too much lard and cocoa   but makes strawberry
from the box for my birthday the year I ask

he lets me crack the eggs

TELL ME

EVERYTHING I KNOW.

Tell me
         again,
         slower this time.

Tell me
         not to be afraid
                 of all this living left to do;

         that death is just the shades drawn,
                 a cool washcloth, jersey sheets:
                 the color of coffee with cream.

Kindly tell me
         how to be; write it by hand.
                 Put it all in a letter that
                 gets lost in the mail.

CREATIVE
NONFICTION

WÜSTHOF SILVERPOINT II 10-PIECE SET

I pulled a knife from the block, my favorite chopping knife with its blunt tip, round and snub-nosed, though, I'm not sure anyone else could pick it out by that description, but I always know it when I see it because it's my favorite, with its smooth, black handle and the sharpener, too, in its little hole, and I can hear his voice in my ear like a father, like a bladesmith, saying, *Keep them sharp or else they're useless,* and showing me the way to hold the sharpener vertically in one hand, its tip pointing up at the pockmarked ceiling of the house we found on Craigslist, with the tip pointing up he held the knife in the other hand, perpendicular to the sharpener, resting the blade against it at the hilt and pulling it toward him then thrusting it forward, over and over again he did this, and the metals together made a *whoosh,* made a *shingg,* the metal shining, catching the yellow kitchen light like a ring would have, like the ring the knives were supposed to be, on my finger, the left hand, the hand I'd use to hold the sharpener, the hand where nothing sparkled even after the words *two years, big gift, something special;* the knives are in a different home now, my home with someone who isn't him, and when I packed my things I wondered if they were mine to take because it never really felt they were for me in the first place, after all, did I even care enough to sharpen them, *Come here and let me show you, When's the last time you sharpened these, Too long, too long, Look how it won't even cut through the skin of this lime, Too long, Watch how I sharpen it, Now it goes right through, see,* and so we made drinks and we talked, and I miss those talks where I could say something exactly, or close, and he would understand the thing exactly, or if he didn't, would talk through and around and over and over again until he did, and by the end I knew I understood it better too, and we would make love against the kitchen counter, on the chaise lounge, on the hood of the car in the open-air garage because the neighbors were old and already asleep; the man made hunting knives out of his shed, sharpened them on a big wheel in the big shed behind his garden, his garden which was so much better than our garden and that summer while I was watering our cherry tomatoes he handed me a basket of cucumbers and I didn't know they would be prickly, that they didn't want to be held by me or the old man or his wife who was in and out of the hospital and never heard us on the hood of the car because she went to bed around eight and her husband shortly after, but he knew how to sharpen a knife and grow a garden and keep a wife for fifty-plus years, and I should've asked him how to sharpen a knife because sometimes it's hard to learn from the people we love, and how to grow a garden because the squirrels kept eating my peppers, squirrels with pepper breath, and how to keep a wife for fifty-plus years because maybe then I could've told him how to keep me, and he never would've said, *So you really don't think you'll regret this,* and I never would have looked back at him sitting on our green, tweed couch, *If you walk out that door it's over,* and me with one foot out the door saying, *I know,* and then closing the door and driving past the cheese factory that pumped cheddar into the air and the grocery store where we bought things to chop, things that dulled the knives, and then driving back three days later while he was at work and packing everything, including the two-year knife set, into a trailer attached to a truck that drove me away from the tweed couch and the spent garden and the love that taught me how to sharpen things.

GENTLE CARE VETERINARY CLINIC
PET EUTHANASIA CONSENT FORM

Date: 03/03/2016

Owner's Name: Brenna Womer; though, I can't help but feel she's Neil's too, still. Maybe it's because he chipped in half the money to have her spayed. Maybe it's the memory of him washing her in a Rubbermaid bin on our back porch, wearing the threadbare button-up I bought him at a thrift store, his bare feet stuck with bits of dead grass. It's been over two years since I left, since he and I have spoken, but we got Danza together, and, if it were me, I would want to know.

Patient's Name: Danza (Tiny Danza, Danza Brown, Danny, Danny Doo, Danzalina, Bean, Beany, Danza Bean, Punk, Punky Brewster, Punky Rooster, Baby Girl)

Owner's Address: In a loft that's too big for just me since the last guy moved out — he and I were never going to work. We ran out of things to talk about on our second date and spent a year in silence, playing on our phones. He was allergic to dogs, so my parents took Danza; now sometimes Dad calls me by her name. When Neil and I got her she was so small, five-pounds tiny. We had a house and a life and a love that worked, a love that felt like love. Not all of it does, you know? Some of it feels like loyalty or guilt or laziness; sometimes it only feels like reciprocation. He and I drove to Birch Tree, Missouri and met a woman from Pet Finder in front of a gas station built to look like a log cabin just off the highway, two hours from home. Our home.

Microchip number: I never did have hers activated, though I would absent-mindedly push at the pill-shaped lump just under her pink skin and short hair, little body covered in eyelashes, during movie nights on the green, tweed couch we found at the Salvation Army.

Age: Three, barely. We had been together for a year and a half when we got her, just eight weeks old — a companion for Neil's scruffy rat terrier, Wedge. We only lasted another year, because you know when you're 21 and, even when things are good, you assume there's better buried somewhere you haven't looked?

Species/Breed: The woman handed me this barrel-chested curl, warm but shaking from the rain and January cold. A dachshund she'd found in a trashcan and named Treasure, because one man's trash.	Sex: Sweet baby girl, pees with her crotch to the dirt. She never knew her sex, stitches in her overripe peach of a belly.
Weight: I don't know anymore, I guess. Mom and Dad have a tendency to overfeed. There's a layer of fat now over her long ribcage, rolls at her neck, and her stomach is a soft, sagging paunch.	Color: Brown everything, just like me.

Would you like a necropsy (autopsy) to determine COD? I know the cause — another slipped disc. Shit started slipping, and she went numb. The medication's run out but didn't seem to do much for the pain anyway. There is no cure and even if she gets better this time the chances are it'll happen again, so this is it. She can't keep living like this.

I ask my animal's remains be cared for in the following way: You gave me a paper with my options — return of body for home burial, cremation and return of ashes, cremation and disposal of ashes, or, simply, disposal — and I don't know which to choose because I'm running out of Neil. The paper-thin pint glass we brought back from Kansas City cracked in the dishwasher, right through the little crown etched below the lip. The rose in the drained bottle of Irony Cabernet from our last Valentine's together snapped in half on the window sill when I drew the blinds. The house his sister sold, where we danced to "Call Me Al," drunk, in the kitchen after the Super Bowl, the one where his brother-in-law proposed at half-time and we all cried as Bruno Mars danced across the screen in a gold suit jacket, Panza hiding in the lining of the couch for all the excitement. I don't have much left of him that I can hold onto, but ashes might be worse than nothing. And there isn't any home to take her back to. Not any more.

Brenna G Womac

(Signature)

MOTHERLODE

I want to be a mother but only on Sundays, yelling at them not to dirty their best in the woods behind the church. French Roast Folgers, Styrofoam cups, single serving Coffee-mate creamers, and Sweet'N Low packets that cause cancer like microwaves and cellphones, but we use them anyway because God is in control. I layer Oreo crumbs, Jell-O pudding, and Cool Whip in hand-me-down Pyrex for the potluck after second service. Don't doodle in the hymnal; shirttail tucked; eyes closed when we pray; take the grape juice from the inner circle—the wine is for Mommy; don't eat the bread, *the body*, before Pastor blesses it.

I want to be a mother when she has ballet at the little studio downtown; when his number is painted on my cheek for Friday night football; during the hour we spend making brownies and then licking the bowl, and in the thirty seconds it takes them to tear through their Christmas Eve stockings.

I want to be a mother, but only during the in-between times when I'm not fucking it up. When I'm not giving them a reason to hate me, hate the world, hate themselves. Early on, when they're fresh things, in those quiet night hours as they feed from my body, looking at me or past me—my connection to the realm of spirits, to God the Father, the Mother. My portal to a higher, better place before they learn to be here, to be human.

I want to be a mother before my daughter learns what she is to the world, before she gets angry at me for telling her the way things are, for breaking that beautiful spell as my own mother did. Before she spreads her legs for the first, the could-be, the why-won't-you, the true, the broken, and the anything-to-fill-this-hole kinds of love. We are not princesses.

I want to be a mother before I hate my son for what's between his legs: the soft, pillowy flesh he'll learn to wield like a sword. Let me be a mother before he realizes the power he has. Before boys will be boys and all guys do it and that's just the way men are. When he's brand new and sliding out of me, when he's latched on and drinking, when he bathes with his sister and kisses her on the mouth—before the world teaches them their place.

I want to be a mother, because I'm supposed to want to be a mother. But as I sat waiting for the nurse to come back with pregnancy-test results, a picture of two kids in a cornfield taped to her name badge, it wasn't a choice. It wasn't want. It was a thing that was happening, like an earthquake or daylight saving time. And even if I decided to say *No, no thank you* or *Not now, not yet*—even if I slept through the quake and refused to set my clocks back—still, forever, once, I was a mother. I was the one who would love and ruin them, the one they'd respect and blame. I was the one who'd know their bodies first, their minds, before they knew themselves, and keep their secrets before they understood there were any to keep. With a cocktail of fear and want, no and yes, me and all their potential in my belly, I was—for however brief a time—Mother.

MALE DOCTORS & MY ANATOMY

I.

His fingers are freckled and hairy and sausage-thick, and he waits until he's palpating my ovaries to ask how classes are going.

You're almost done now, hey?

He's been asking this question since I was a senior in high school. Now in the second year of my Master's, I just say

Yep

because I don't like the way my body tightens around his fingers when I speak.

Your grandparents came into town for a checkup just last week, he says.

He tells me to untie the front of my gown and raise my arms.

Try to touch the ceiling, he says.

He breathes, hot and wet, into cupped hands before fingering my breasts the way a child bangs their way up and down a piano in feigned familiarity.

They're good people, he says, but I've forgotten who he's talking about.

II.

He's wearing blue jeans.

Does it smell like a can of tunafish? he asks, and I hate that he says "tuna fish" like it's one word.

I see my mother draining albacore in water over the sink for casserole night, pressing the metal lid into dry, flaky meat. Juice squirts and drips.

No, I say. (I lie.)

His phone buzzes in its holster, and he holds up a finger; he takes the call. He presses a few buttons and then hangs up.

It was a survey, he says.

He diagnoses me without lifting up my gown, because, at this point, we both hate my tunafish cunt.

III.

He draws a house and a stoop and a path to the front gate, to the curbside mailbox.

He draws a stick figure one step down from the door.

This is you, he says, pointing to the stick.

The house is healthy, and the mailbox is cervical cancer. I'm trying to keep you from checking the mail.

He hands me the drawing.

For your fridge, he says.

IV.

He tells me to

Lean back, feet in the stirrups. Scoot-your-boot down to the edge of the table.

He tells me to

Relax.

The scope is large and white and attached to an arm like an optometry phoropter, but this doctor is looking for precancerous cells so much smaller than letters at the bottom of an eye chart.

I'll be swabbing your cervix with a hand-mop soaked in vinegar, he says.

Think of it like I'm making a salad in your vagina.

When he's finished, he shakes my hand and leaves me with a pamphlet that warns of post-procedure stench and spotting and cramps. That tells me not to be alarmed by the deposit of a thick, black scab in a day or two. I put my underwear back on; I wash my hands.

FOREVER BLONDE

We were together for a summer, the first one he'd ever spent away from his two little girls who were downstate with their mother. He called her *my ex* on our first couple of dates and then *Nicole* for a handful after that, but it wasn't long before she was back to being *Nic*—a name I thought too endearing for someone he was trying not to love anymore.

On Saturdays we'd stay in pajamas and play cribbage at the dining room table. He'd make mug after mug of pour-over coffee, and at some point I'd go to the guest bathroom to take a shit, nothing to look at but family photos. I learned that Nicole had homebirths and breastfed and that there was no chance he'd ever look at either of their beautiful girls without thinking of her.

Each new thing he learned about me seemed to fall into one of two categories—Like Nicole or Unlike Nicole—and soon he was trying to fix me with the bits of her he had left: old snowshoes so I wouldn't have to buy a pair that winter, too-small tampons under the master bathroom sink, clonazepam in the medicine cabinet in case I forgot to pack my own, and a scalding bath for a UTI because she used to be a nurse and swore by it.

Nic will always be the mother of my children, he'd said, unprompted, more than once. But it got old, feeling him go limp in my mouth when her ringtone played, washing my dark brown hair with the dregs of her Forever Blonde shampoo.

CUKES

Looking down into a bin of cucumbers at the grocery store and call-ing them, with their myriad curves and girths, by the names of men I know or have known—the orgasms I never had but said I did. Ripped foil, latex and non, colors and ribs, lubes and spermicides; rolling skin over slick skin; breaking, slipping, coming off inside of me and falling out two days later like a sitcom tragedy. Pulling thin, soft plastic from a roll overhead, picking a cucumber without a name.

SATE

IV

On my fourth birthday the woman in line behind us at the bakery smelled like sex. It was mid-morning, and half-baked loaves were browning behind glass oven doors. The shop was warm to assist the yeast and gluten, dough rising beneath damp kitchen towels. Before the woman who smelled like sex arrived, the air was light and thick with loose flour and brewed coffee, cinnamon and fresh bread. When she walked in, the scent of the room took a sharp turn for warm water and salt, cumin and bergamot, not so sour as a lemon, but bitter like rind and rust. I didn't know the smell for what it was at the time—sweaty passion dried to olive skin at nape and spine and lower back, the pits of knees; tart, pheromone spice under arms and between thighs. If there had been a plant in the room it would have wilted. I wondered if the dough would still be able to rise with such an atmospheric shift, and, if it did rise, whether the bread it made might taste like her too.

My mother pulled me close to her side and handed me a tissue.

Cover your nose and mouth with this, she said, *like a mask*, and proceeded to cover her own just the same. But I liked the smell and lifted a corner of the tissue to breathe it in.

The baker acknowledged the woman and then asked how old I was as she poured whole milk into a bowl of powdered sugar. Whisking the extra glaze for my birthday cinnamon roll, she watched as my mother bent my right thumb into my right palm and held up my hand by the wrist. My mother lifted the bottom of her tissue so we could see her mouthing the word *four*, and I could feel the arch of her over-plucked brows as she anticipated my own recitation of the number for the baker. But I was watching the woman in line behind us.

Her dress was pale yellow, thin cotton, and wrinkled from a handful of hours on the floor. She carried her sandals and a book under one arm; there was a little tattoo—of what, I can't recall—at the ankle of one of her bare feet. She winked when she saw me staring, to which I snapped my head down and noted, as my mother made plug-nosed chit-chat with the baker, my own shoes on the wrong feet, the tips curving away from each other like a fork in the road.

When I looked back up at the woman, indulging curiosity, she was still looking at me. We had the same pageboy haircut, and so she said, as she mussed up her own with a free hand, *I like your hair.*

I smiled under my tissue.

We watched, the three of us in line, as the baker drizzled thick frost from the cage of the whisk over a single roll—my special, once-a-year, birthday breakfast.

Can you dress one more of those, please, while you're at it? asked the woman who smelled like sex.

My mother curled the lip of the white paper sack and handed it to me, not to be eaten until we got home to plate and fork and damp napkin, a plastic baggy for the leftovers she'd make certain I'd have, telling me when I was full instead of letting me feel the ache and stretch and sick of it for myself.

As my mother poured cream into her coffee, everything taking her a bit longer than usual with just one free hand, the woman who smelled like sex ate her cinnamon roll from a square of parchment paper at a table for two, her feet up and resting on the opposite chair. She took bites so big she couldn't chew them with her mouth closed and ate without regard for the frosting at her upper lip. The sealed curl of the paper bag that held my own roll was turning damp, the fibers weakening in my overwrought clench.

Before my mother had finished saying goodbye to the baker, the woman who smelled like sex—on what appeared to be, for her, a most ordinary morning—having disappeared an iteration of my very special, once-a-year, birthday breakfast, brushed crusted sugar from tabletop to floor and left the shop, with no particular sense of urgency.

VII

I couldn't sleep, so I left the guest bed my mother and I were sharing and turned on *Full House* in my grandparents' living room. My grandfather had already switched off the lighted magnifying glass over his stamp collection and had retired from his desk for the night. With my thighs stuck to their brown leather couch, my great-grandmother's hideous scrap afghan over my lap, it was then I had an itch where I'd never had an itch before, an itch that, in the scratching, led to a new sensation altogether. Scratching turned to rubbing, which settled into a comfortable rhythm that seemed, somehow, deeply familiar—muscle memory without the memory itself. With the Tanners watching from the television nightlight, my hand moved in a way it had been waiting to move, fingering keys and hammering strings, the pumping of feet on the pedalboard. I could hear the music of a pipe organ, just one rank at first, quietly, and then another—a familiar Sunday school song:

It was on a Monday somebody touched me; it was on a Monday somebody touched me; it was on a Monday somebody touched me; it must've been the hand of The Lord.

The music played on, building, through Tuesday and Wednesday and Thursday. In church we were supposed to stand on the day we were saved, but because I couldn't remember the day, the moment, I denied my flesh and became a creature of the Spirit, I stood on Sunday. The organ beat on in a weekend crescendo, and my toes pointed the way I'd learned in the ballet class I'd quit after two weeks; I reared my chin into my neck and arched my back, and it was then I saw my mother in the doorway.

XI

The Altus Air Force Base Community Activities Committee got the idea to stock a decommissioned swimming pool with lake water and trout for kids to catch, so many fish you couldn't drop a line in without catching one. Looking down at the water, you could see them flopping over each other, too many bodies, too many walls. I went with my father. He hated fish but liked taking me to these sorts of events.

I'd had my first period the month before, a sudden damp between my legs while my mother and I browsed at the Christian bookstore. I'm sure she had told my father, but he hadn't said anything about it to me. And now we were fishing. The limit was three, which I caught in three casts, deriving little satisfaction from the lack of effort, of mystery. We took my fish to the cleaning station where men from my father's squadron waited with fillet knives at a table next to the defunct lifeguard stand. One of them slid his hooknosed knife the length of the first fish's stomach, and at once I felt the dull hook-and-snag of a seam ripper deep inside my own, a spasmodic roiling as the man reached inside to loose a mess of slick string and organs with a bloodied glove.

This one was a lady, the man said, scraping peach roe from its swollen gut. *You want the eggs, Chief*, he asked my father, who made a face that answered no.

With that, the man slid his knife-edge along the table and pushed the eggs into the trash bin at the end. I could feel the hot red wet at my inner thigh and told my dad I had to pee.

IXX

I hadn't yet felt the raw slick of him inside of me. He said:

I just don't think we can experience the full spectrum *of intimacy with something synthetic between us. The barrier is kind of like a metaphor, don't you think?*

He took off his pants, always black-turned-brown at the thighs and back pockets from espresso he ground and tamped and poured part-time for me and the other hundred college students who wandered into the coffee shop each day. He was five years older, handsome, elusive, and graduated, an illustrator always sketching people uglier than they were in real life. Eventually he and I would move in together, and for two years he would insist we wash our clothes in separate loads of laundry.

It had been a week since I requested a prescription for the pill, a week since my doctor asked me to recall the Elmer's glue I'd used in grade school, how it might piece together one of the lives waiting to live or die inside of me.

Always use backup, he'd said. *This is no guarantee.*

The barista, in boxer briefs, pulled off his black-brown v-neck.

It's the difference between fucking and making love, he said, and I stared at his wide, pepperoni nipples.

I wanted to know if, when he came, I'd feel it inside like spray from a garden hose, like the chocolate gush from a molten lava cake. If maybe the glue might piece together more than someone else inside of me. And so we fucked for the first time without anything between us.

It was six pumps before, *I'm coming*—syllables flaking from his lips like soup crackers: *Baby, baby, baby.*

When he rolled off me his dick slapped wet against my thigh, and he put his hand on mine. Smiling, sweaty, he said, *You don't wanna wait long to clean up. It'll run right out of you.*

The only thing I hadn't expected was for it to feel like nothing at all.

XXX

I'll turn thirty at 12:07 PM, and they'll start to fall, all of them at once, eggs in a 7-Eleven bathroom. The first one will plop into the bowl, followed by another, and then two, out of me like raw, peeled shrimp. Two at a time, then three and four together, and soon the bowl will be full. I'll stand up, half-naked, with eggs falling to the tiled floor. In a panic, I'll scoop them from the toilet and fill the wastebasket, but they'll start falling half-a-dozen at a time and I won't be able to keep up. I'll cup them into the sink, mashing them to the sides with my fist, mortar and pestle, pressing them down the open drain, pulp between my fingers and under my nails. Hundreds, and then thousands, so I'll stop, ankle-deep, and let them fall. Globules the size of gumballs, clear and gelatinous, pink and blue veins running through, some with sprouts of hair and chips of teeth at their centers. When the line approaches my knees, they'll start to slow, like popping corn in the microwave. I'll wade through them for my purse atop the tank, squish my hands through the mess for the pants at my feet. When I heave the door open, they'll spill out into the aisles of corn chips and condoms and chocolate-covered peanuts, and a woman not much older than myself will lift her child from the ground, hold its face to her own in horror.

With eggs in my shoes, trapped in the crotch of my underwear, I'll walk for the register and try to remember whether I was the baker or the mother or the daughter or the woman who smelled like sex.

Hypochondria, or The Disease

arrhythmia, *n.*

Want of **rhythm** or regularity; *spec.* of the pulse.

⌞Two fingers at wrist or neck: *I am, I am, I am.* Before **diagnoses**; the old bray
of my **heart** to remind me, still, I exist.   ⌞**anxiety; panic**

⌞skips beats, but only before **orgasm**; only   **disorder; depression.**
while kneading dough.   ⌞"We'd have to   ⌞Lexapro; Klonopin;
get your boy-   Paxil; Ambien.
friend in here
to test out that theory," the doctor said.
A joke—I laughed. Thought, *No, we
really wouldn't.*

bacterial vaginosis, *n.*

Bacterial overgrowth in the **vagina**.

⌞Prescribed: clindamycin.   ⌞**he** doesn't examine before diagnosis.

⌞the old man in blue jeans, no lab coat; shadowed by a
young man, nervous, with a **clipboard**.

⌞shuffles papers while the
doctor takes a **phone call**
on his cell.   ⌞It's an
automated
survey

⌐is right.

⌐"You don't have *fucking* carpal tunnel," **he** says, letting our breakfast burn in the pan.

carpal tunnel syndrome, *n.*

Median nerve compression in the wrist's carpal tunnel, characterized by a burning or tingling pain in the hand, sometimes with **sensory loss** and muscle weakness, associated with work that involves **repetitive movements.**   └for **days** I can't feel my hands.

└A part-time job frosting   └after the first **attack**.

cupcakes; the signature swirl.   └"Panic," the
                                                   doctor says.
                                                   "A disorder."

deep vein thrombosis, *n.*

(or DVT) a **blood clot** in a deep vein, usually in the legs.

└**Birth control** increases a woman's risk by three to four times.

└**because** he can't come when he's wearing a condom.

└**he** hates it when there's anything between us.

└**would** take a pill if there were one for men.

└**pay** for an **abortion** if it ever came to that.

└$350-$650 └pill; vacuum aspiration; dilation & evacuation.

early-onset Alzheimer's disease, *n.*

A type of **dementia** that causes problems with memory, thinking, and behavior. Symptoms usually   └Nanny **Betty**, my father's mother, who doesn't know who I am anymore.
develop slowly   └my middle name, Elizabeth, for **her**.
and worsen over time   └blood is mine.
becoming severe enough to interfere with **daily tasks**.

                    └bringing a cup to my mouth without spilling.
                    └punching in the code for our apartment door.
                    └remembering the word for *pen*.
                    └buttoning my shirt.

⌈left arm.

⌈Rarely, a person may develop GBS in the days or weeks after receiving the **flu shot.**

Guillain-Barré syndrome, *n.*

An acute form of peripheral nerve damage often preceded by a respiratory infection and the most common cause of ascending **paralysis.**

⌞No sleep, and I can't feel my feet—numb and soft and dead as dough, but I know not to wake him for this. He doesn't like the **new** me.

⌞scared

⌞**weak**

⌞"You should be stronger than this."

⌞**crazy**

⌞"It's like you're a different person."

⌞"I can't do life like this."

⌈I Learned the Hard Way

⌈garbage

⌈No One Told Me

⌈rebound

⌈list: **Things** My Mother Should've Told Me

human papillomavirus, *n.*   ⌈that condoms **don't protect** against.

(or HPV) A group of over **150 viruses, each** assigned its own **number,**

that can lead to cancers of the mouth,   ⌞strain   ⌞**High-risk:** 16 & 18

throat, anus, rectum, penis, **cervix,** vagina,   ⌞31, 33, 45, 52, & 58.

and vulva, though most   ⌞**cervical cancer**

cases of HPV **disappear**   ⌞the leading cause.

on their own.   ⌞like my mother's when she was 19.

⌞**like mine** at 23.

⌞but **not before** five pap smears in two years.   ⌈LEEP: Loop

⌞**colposcopy** for biopsy; talk of **cauterization.**   Electrosurgical

↓   ⌞risks: bleeding   Excision

Greek | Procedure

↓   infection

"to look at a hollow womb." |

infertility

74

hypochondriasis, *n.*

Chiefly characterized by the patient's unfounded belief that she is suffering from some serious bodily disease; characterized by a morbid preoccupation with one's bodily health together with unfounded beliefs and exaggerated anxieties of **real** or imagined ailments, usually the symptom of a neurotic disorder. ⌊**always**
⌊to me.

mad cow, *n.*

(or bovine spongiform encephalopathy) A fatal disease in cattle that causes degeneration of the brain and spinal cord. When transferred to humans, it is called variant Creutzfeldt-Jakob disease, and the **United Kingdom** was the country most affected by the **epidemic**, from 1986-1998. ⌊2001: FDA restricts blood donations from any people residing longer than three months in the UK **after 1980**. ⌊They will not take my blood for what might lie in wait, **dormant**.

⌊1992: Bury St. Edmunds, birthplace.
⌊1996-2000: RAF Mildenhall, resident.

⌊Incubation period: unknown.

⌐me　　　　　　　⌐"It's *very* unlikely," the doctor says.
⌐with **someone** who has **HPV**.
⌐**sex**　　　　　　　　　　⌐mine, after he's been inside me.
oral cancer, *n*　　　　　　└his, between my legs.
　　A **cancer** that develops in any part of the **mouth**.
　　　　└"What about **Michael Douglas**?" I ask.
　　　　　└the doctor says, "is full of shit."

before birth
　↑　　　↑
prae⊤gnasci
　Latin　　　　　　　　　　　　　　⌐you never discussed.
　　↑　　　　　　　　　　　　　⌐"**deal**-breaker"
pregnancy, *n.*　　　　　　　⌐"What if **I don't want** one?"
　　The **condition** of a **female** of being pregnant or with **child**; a(n) **instance** of this.
　　　　└assumed　　　↓　　　　　　　└*n.* urgent entreaty or
　　　　　　　　　Latin → **femina**　　　　**solicitation**.
　　　　　　　　　└a **woman**　　　　　　└*n.* the act of trying to
　　　　　　　　　　　↓　　　　　　　　　　obtain something
　　　　　　　　Old English　　　　　　　　from someone.
　　　　　　　　wīf└mon
　　　　　　　　　↓　　↓
　　　　　　　　wife man
　　　　　　　　└inherent

　　　　　⌐SADS
　　　⌐**adult**
sudden infant death syndrome, *n.*
　　(or SIDS) The unexplained **death**, usually during **sleep**, of a seemingly healthy baby less
　　than a year old.　　　　└They don't wake　└no **sleep**,
　　　　　　　　　　　　　up when they　　　└but I try for it, on my back, the
　　　　　　　　　　　　　stop **breathing**.　　week I learn.
　　　　　　　　　　　　└It's harder for the
　　　　　　　　　　　　lungs to fill and lift the
　　　　　　　　　　　　body when lying face-down.

trauma, *n.* ⌈ *adj.* relating to the soul or mind.

    A **psychic** injury, esp. caused by emotional shock, the **memory** of which is **repressed** and
    remains unhealed.
           ↓

        Latin
    re-⌋   ⌊manere
     ↓   ↓
again & again, to stay

                                      ⌊Lipton iced tea   ⌊
                                        powder mix
                                      ⌊late afternoon
                                        through living
                                        room **curtains**
                                              ⌊closed
                                    ⌊a babysitter
                                     without a face
                                        ⌊a body
                                    ⌊carpet and wood

Empire Blue

Fort Monroe, Virginia, 2003

We drove in the day before Hurricane Isabel with our lives blocking the rear view of our Ford Expedition. There was no available housing on Langley Air Force Base, so we were assigned to a duplex on Fort Monroe, a neighboring Army base. Fort Monroe is an island in the Chesapeake Bay connected by a short bridge to the Virginia mainland. Our little home was two stories of crumbling red brick, and after the hurricane washed saltwater over the island, everything green turned brown or gray. We would turn back and drive inland to ride out the storm, but not before standing on the seawall together, Mom, Dad, and I, to watch a fleet of Naval ships and submarines from Norfolk set out toward the horizon, for safety.

My mother grew up the middle child of a poor Navy family, and from the time she was born, she moved every two years. She was shy and fearful, the worst-case-scenario for a perpetual new girl. She said she wore dresses too short, even by 1970s standards, because new ones cost money her parents didn't have. Her father was a harsh man—a submariner, a pipe smoker, and a hothead. He was absent throughout her childhood, far more than my father from my own, which left her working mother greatly burdened with three children and a house to keep. Growing up, I wondered at my grandmother's grim mouth and vacant eyes in old photographs because the woman I knew was quick to laugh, full of warmth and kindness. I would learn her sepia-toned gaze was one of an eighth-grade dropout who married a sailor at fifteen to get away from an abusive, alcoholic father. It was the face of a woman who married a man with a short fuse, a man out to sea nine months of every year, a man who kept her pregnant through her late teens and early twenties. Precious years of independence, of self-discovery, lost to swollen ankles and crying babies and dinner on the table every night at five-thirty.

If you asked me what I wanted to be, from the time I was a little girl until my freshman year of college, I would have told you I wanted to be a homemaker. Grandma worked various jobs to help support a struggling household, and when I was growing up my mother worked periodically to help with credit card payments or to stave off a restlessness that still plagues her to this day. But ultimately, their lives were their children; they were homemakers. My mother's side of the family is devoutly religious—Baptist mostly—and they subscribe to Old Testament views on where a woman's value lies—in the home she keeps and the food she makes, in her children, which are her crowning glory, and in the respect she has for her husband who is the head of the household. As I transitioned into my sophomore year of college, I chose to abandon the Christian faith in which I had been raised and did my best to toss off the Southern Baptist ideologies so deeply engrained in my being. With that abandonment came many changes, including a newfound understanding of myself as a singular person, an individual without a preordained path laid out for her. For the first time my life was mine and not something I was living to honor someone else with, and while that was exhilarating, it also instigated a passionate revolt against the life my mother and grandmother had settled into. I was—am—terrified of being owned. By a god or a man or a child or a place. By anyone or anything but myself.

RAF Lakenheath, England, 1999

It was the summer of butterflies. Monarchs and painted ladies, I would later learn, but to us they were the common and uncommon butterflies, respectively. I was seven, and my friends and I spent hours catching them in whatever containers our moms let us take from the kitchen cabinets. Mine was an empty Ragu jar, the label scrubbed clean off for a full view, with holes Mom tapped into the metal lid using a Phillip's head and a hammer from Dad's olive drab, military-issue tool bag. It was my family's last summer on RAF Lakenheath, an Air Force base 80 miles north of London, and the butterfly bush in our front yard smelled sweet and delicate, like the trellis of honeysuckle over my grandparents' porch in San Diego, like the sprig of jasmine a boyfriend's Sri Lankan mother would one day tuck behind my ear.

The *Buddleja davidii*, or Empire Blue, is a cultivar heavy with cone-shaped clusters of tiny purple flowers interspersed between narrow, soft green leaves. Some know the bush as we did, a butterfly bush.

They attract hummingbirds and bees as well, but we only ever saw butterflies. The bushes grow to be about five feet tall and wide, but I remember getting lost inside of it, thick as a cornfield, stalks towering above our heads so high we couldn't see our houses, so dense with purple and green we had to call out to each other, *Any luck?* The *Buddleja davidii* takes so easily to most soils that in Australia and parts of the U.S. it's considered a weed—a fragrant, seductive trespasser. It's known to thrive in areas of disruption. You can find it in a roadside ditch next to fast food cups and candy wrappers, among the rocks on a craggy mountain path, pushing through the tired cracks of a land made barren by fire; your hook might catch in its leaves as you reel in a line from the riverbank. If cut down to a stump at the end of its flowering season, it will come back fuller the following year.

In the shadows of the living room, what was left of the evening light deigning through our sliding glass doors, I asked where my mother was. It was not usual for Dad to pick me up from wherever I had been. He did not like the question, more probably did not like the answer, was not used to telling me the hard things.

"Your mother is in the hospital. She'll be there for a couple weeks."

Why?

"She's just a little sad right now."

Why?

"That's what she's trying to figure out, sweetheart."

We learned it was best to approach butterflies from behind, where we figured we were out of their line of vision, and to make a V with the lid and rim of the container. Once we were close enough to the creature slowly lowering its wings and folding them up together again, showing in turn its beauty and banality, we clapped the lid tight to the container, trapping the butterfly inside. We watched them panic, observed the colors and shapes on their wings until they calmed down and stood at the base of the container with their wings closed in silent protest against our curious stares; how warped and fish-eyed we must have looked through the curvature of the glass. When they were still and showed to us only the muddled underside of their wings, we released them back into the bush for another one of us to catch.

I remember only one visit while she was in the hospital; she took me to the art therapy room and showed me a ceramic trivet she made. She pulled it out of a little cubbyhole and we sat in plastic chairs with metal, hairpin legs—the same we had at Lakenheath Elementary. It was a mosaic of Persian blue and crimson tiles pressed into white grout, and I told her it was beautiful. I remember her in a white hospital gown peppered with pale blue dots, but she was probably wearing jeans and a T-shirt. When she came home it was all the same to me, everything was as it should be. I didn't know the reason she was sad was because she couldn't bring herself to leave my father, and I didn't know the reason she couldn't leave him was because I loved him too much, loved him enough for the both of us. *You were the glue.* The trivet has been on the kitchen counter in every home we've lived in since. It's on their counter now, stained with sauce from jars of Ragu and chipped because I'm clumsy like my mother. Yes, I am my mother's daughter.

***

Six months we lived on the little island of Fort Monroe. My parents' bedroom window looked out onto the bay and the sound of rushing water was constant; it was the silence. I was seven and had taken to collecting sea glass along the shore. By the end of our time there we had drawers full of glass—browns and greens mostly, a handful of blues and pinks. When winter came, I didn't know snow would blanket the sand, would saddle up and ride the waves like rodeo cowboys. I bundled up and looked for frosted chips of glass in the cold, clumped sand. I stuffed them into my pockets, their edges smooth, their surfaces almost fuzzy. They had been opaqued by decades of movement along the ocean floor. Glass beautified in its travels, refined into something desired, less common; a token of a place, of a memory.

I've always known my mother as a rebel, sensed in her a relentless urge to buck tradition, to tell whomever it was holding her to some preordained standard that they could go fuck themselves. She dropped out of high school and married her first husband at eighteen just to get out of the house. Not for the same reason her own mother had—her family was broken in different ways. My mother's first husband was a quiet man, a mechanic. She hasn't told me much about him, or perhaps there just isn't much to tell, simple as he seemed to be. He was an extra in the movie *Hamburger Hill*, and somewhere Mom still has a picture of him with Tom Cruise on the set of *Born on the Fourth of July*. After a year of marriage she enlisted in the Air Force, and a few years after that they got a divorce. She says when they were married she was restless and immature. She says she broke his heart. With this I understand I am her daughter and I think of the e.e. cummings tattoo on my right arm. I think maybe "[i carry your heart with me(i carry it in my]" was not at all about a lover but about a mother. That maybe it's her heart I carry and the deepest secret nobody knows, not even me, is that whatever I do is her doing. Maybe she was the small voice in the dark whispering, *There's more than this. Don't get comfortable*, and the loves I ran away from, the men I broke and the homes I left half-empty, were because her heart is there next to mine in syncopated rhythm asking me to be better, to do it right this time.

Mom was stationed in the Philippines when she took up scuba diving in Puerto Galera. When I was a teenager and charm bracelets were in vogue, she gave me a silver charm from her keepsake box. It was a dingy scuba diver in full gear, flippers and arms poised as though propelling itself through the ocean. She told me to take care of it because it was precious, but she wanted me to have it. I lost it after a couple months and even when I noticed it was gone I didn't give it much thought. I didn't realize it was a relic of the small window between my mother's first husband and my father, the only time she's ever really had to herself. I'm not saying my mother was happy during that time; I'm saying I think she was free. She gave me a token of her independence, a charm to protect like a Catholic saint, to protect me from myself. But I didn't know I would need it. How badly I would one day need to be reminded that I was my own, that I was enough. That I didn't need anyone to tell me I existed for it to be true. Mom never asked about the charm or looked for it on my bracelet, though she usually keeps a close eye on things she or the family gives to me, things of sentimental value. It was like she passed a torch and then hurried to forget the flame, now my burden to bear.

Altus AFB, Oklahoma, 2001

There were no *Buddleja davidii* on Altus Air Force Base, and not many butterflies either as I recall; maybe they despised the Oklahoma heat as much as my mother did. A shallow creek was the dividing line between enlisted and officer housing, the flowers and the trees; we lived on Honeysuckle Avenue. The Altus outside of the base gates was one of Friday night lights and Bulldog pride, smoky restaurants and beauty parlors, white T-shirts and coveralls. We went to church at First Baptist and out for lunch at Subway after, to Hastings for books and movie rentals, and to Moonlight Music for my weekly guitar lesson with Mr. Eddy. In the dry heat from the sun we shared with Texas, I practiced John Denver's "Country Roads" and Patty Loveless' "Chains" in our one-car garage until little calluses formed behind the nails on my left hand. Altus was where Dad bought our purple, hail-dented Kia Sephia with the CD player he fed *Juke Box Jive* on our weekend drives for snow cones—the stand run by high school girls with long, blond ponytails who looked so different from me at age nine, with my brown everything and belly like the Laughing Buddha, they made me ache long before I finished my tropical ice.

I suspected I wasn't beautiful. Beauty seemed to eat less, take longer to lose its breath, and wear something other than a one-piece to the pool. At the time I thought I wasn't allowed to wear a bikini because they were immodest. We were Southern Baptist, and bikinis rivaled the scandal of VHS tapes rated PG and above, the ones my parents would feel convicted about and, as a consolation, let me smash to pieces in the driveway with a hammer. For my eighth birthday, I got a pink bikini in the mail from my grandparents, and because it was a present I knew I could talk my mother into letting me wear it. When I asked her, she was hesitant as I had anticipated, but she didn't say anything about modesty. Instead, she winced, and said without saying, *You're going to have to learn this the hard way*.

When I got to the base pool the next day I felt beauty radiating from under my cover-up. The bikini. I was there with my father who had set himself up to tan on a plastic folding chair. My mother never came with us, not that I can remember, and I suspect it was because she didn't want her body contrast next to his. Dad's only hobby was exercising. He was lean with defined abs and biceps, and he effortlessly executed the somersault-dive combo off the diving board—the envy of every showboat teenage boy in the place. How easily he caught their attention. Dad would binge on bags of mini Twix and Three Musketeers after dinner each night in front of the television and then run it off the next day. My mother bounced between diets, sneaking fun-size candies from his bags; I can't remember a time when she didn't hate her body. She resented him for how easy he made it look, for all the dinners she made him that she wasn't allowed to eat, for the way he sculpted his body while she was sharpening her mind and that it didn't matter how many books she read or Styrofoam containers she delivered for Meals On Wheels or how good of mother she was to me, she'd still catch him checking out the tall blond a few lanes down during their bowling league on Tuesday nights—*You see that woman over there? She's exactly your father's type.*

It was a rule to rinse off before getting in the pool, and so I emerged from the ladies' locker room in my new suit with my hair slicked back, Lycra clinging to my chest. My chest, which was not filling out quite as amply as the dark hairs poking out from my bikini bottoms. I sucked in my stomach, creating an unnatural cave beneath my ribcage. I placed a hand at my waist and tried not to accentuate my wide, Latina hips—destined to be referred to as "childbearing." I walked past a table of middle school boys, scrawny and pale with backward caps, drinking cans of Surge from the soda machine. I walked slowly and made eye contact with a boy at the center of the group, the skin at my thighs like Jell-o pudding with each step. He scrunched his nose, and a look of distaste mutated into a wry smile before my plain brown eyes. He turned and laughed with the boy next to him. I looked down at my stomach, which was impeding the view of my thighs, and felt shame hotter than the concrete I scuttled across to the chair where my father was tanning. I covered myself with a towel.

Instead of butterflies, in Altus we caught crawdads, little ones that swam the creek between the flowers and the trees. Our moms netted wire coat hangers with old lace for catching, and when we met at the water it didn't matter whether our dads wore stripes or bars or stars, or who saluted first. The crawdads were harder to catch; they didn't share the air with us and camouflaged against the slimy rocks, disappeared into the moss and mud. I never liked to touch the things I caught. I wanted to look at them, creatures so different from our dogs and gerbils, from myself, yet still alive and breathing. The satisfaction was in the catching, in seeing the crawdad's armor contrast against pale yellow, pincers snagging at the lace. It was cruel to keep them in tanks the way some of my friends did, the butterflies in jars; maybe not if it was all they'd ever known. But to have an endless world replaced by walls and ceilings and stale, sour air was—still is—to me a tragedy of the highest order.

***

When my parents met, they were drunk at the Enlisted Club on Osan Air Base in South Korea. Two months later, they were married and honeymooning in Seoul. Dad was still wounded from a broken engagement to a woman back home in England where he grew up, and Mom's divorce had been final for less than a year. They found companionship in each other, and that was enough for a time. They were stationed apart for a year shortly after they were married. Mom was sent to Hawaii and Dad went back to England.

There's a picture of them on a bed, dating or newlyweds, lying on a plush mink blanket. Dad's hand is lost in her messy brown perm, and they're kissing in a way I've never seen them kiss, in a way I'm not sure they've ever kissed each other since. Two people I have never met. In Hawaii, my mother quit drinking and found Jesus; she quit swearing and the Spirit moved her to speak in tongues. She ran nighttime miles around the lighted flight line to clear her head. My father reconnected with his ex-fiancé and sent my mother a letter he asked her to tear up without opening after a change of heart, which of course she didn't do. I understand I am my mother's daughter. Self-destructive, curious to a fault, distrusting, and fiercely protective of herself—her heart is a guarded thing and my father will never know it wholly. Over twenty-five years together and still there are still folds of her heart too precious to let him see. Corners so dark I wonder if her god can even know them.

She wanted to leave him early on, but the Bible says if the man wants you to stay, you should stay, and he wasn't ready to let her go. My father would rather be unhappy than alone. She didn't re-enlist and moved to England to be with him. He had no interest in changing, no interest in her newfound religion, and so they existed together. *Roommates,* she's said. With the way she talks about that time, I'm not quite sure how it happened, but she found out she was pregnant with me. Me, the glue—*After I found out, that was it. I could never take you away from your father*—the chain that bound her to this life, to him.

Mom says they are happy now, together, and I can see that they are. *I love your dad, and I know he loves me. We're good together,* she says. They have their routines and they look out for each other. Mom still hates to cook, but does it anyway because Dad won't make anything that can't be toasted or microwaved. He buys her flowers once a week and leaves her colorful notes on a whiteboard on the side of the fridge every morning before he goes to the gym. This version of them took me a while to get used to because for most of my childhood I could not understand why they didn't just get a divorce. My mother's bitterness toward my dad was palpable, verbalized to me in moments of desperation and weakness from a young age, and if I was to believe the right person for me was out there somewhere, someone who would make me happy and make me better, then it followed that those people were out there for my parents too. Sometimes my heart still hurts for them because how could they have known how bad it would get before it got better? And then that hurt turns to fear. How can anyone ever know?

***

Skimming the shore for sea glass one gray, November morning, Mom and I found a pair of seagulls caught on two hooks of the same iridescent lure. She sent me back to the house for pliers and when I returned she had me slick one of the bird's wings down tight against its body to hold as she worked the hook from its beak. It thrashed against us, but Mom was able to loose the hook and the bird was left with nothing more than a hole, a little scar for remembering. I released its feathery body onto the sand and it took flight. We continued to work on the second gull, but it didn't fight us like the other one had and was losing a lot of blood. After fifteen minutes of twisting and prying, Mom took up the bird in her slender hands and tossed it onto the rocks, her gold wedding band catching the sunlight over the bay, the gull in total surrender, plastic fish dangling from its mouth.

-cosms

A Response to Nicole Walker's Micrograms

microlove and micropain: microthoughts cordoned in a yogurt brain. microguilt over
microgoats, the blood that blooms from a microthroat. micromoons emitting microlight on a dented hood from a microbike. microsperm on a toilet seat; microlife feeding at a microteet. microwings through the tall, tall trees refusing to bow to the microbreeze. microdeaths turn to microdoubts; ageless thirsts causing microdroughts. microhairs cleaned by microbugs, and spores engorged and microslugs. microstars before white light came, implode by the time we give a microname. microstates painted brilliant blue, the micromiles to get to you. microfear for the microlump and losing hair by the microclump. microweeds through the microcracks by the microstrength of their microbacks. microcones wrapped in plastic bags that were butter-heavy and microsagged. microkin and microfriend making microplans for the microend.

-cosms

A Response to Nicole Walker's Micrograms

microlove and micropain: microthoughts cordoned in a yogurt brain. microguilt over
microgoats, the blood that blooms from a microthroat. micromoons emitting microlight on a dented hood from a microbike. microsperm on a toilet seat; microlife feeding at a microteet. microwings through the tall, tall trees refusing to bow to the microbreeze. microdeaths turn to microdoubts; ageless thirsts causing microdroughts. microhairs cleaned by microbugs, and spores engorged and microslugs. microstars before white light came, implode by the time we give a microname. microstates painted brilliant blue, the micromiles to get to you. micro-fear for the microlump and losing hair by the microclump. microweeds through the microcracks by the microstrength of their microbacks. microcones wrapped in plastic bags that were butter-heavy and micros-agged. microkin and microfriend making microplans for the microend.

We Are Not Saints

A woman I'm not supposed to name offers me donuts and muffin-tin cheesecakes like my mother used to make for Sunday potlucks. She'd let me put the Nilla Wafers at the bottom of the paper liners, but this woman—two years sober, today—says she used graham cracker crumbs. They have coffee in two pots, one with an orange rim and handle, but a man I'm not supposed to name tells me not to mind the colors. *All the same*, he says.

*

My scalp tingles and the Lake is in my ears. At night I hear the waves from my bedroom, but it's three in the afternoon and this is different. They're crashing at my door, at the windows, working to weather this ancient apartment glass into chips of fog.

*

Bob was set to pick up his 15-year chip when he died, not too suddenly, of something that made sense for a man in his 70s who'd started smoking in his early teens and spent a few decades of his life three sheets to the wind. Bob's son, Richard, took him to his first AA meeting, which was fitting, as it was he who, during his teenage years, had borne the brunt of his father's alcoholism. Roger, the oldest, joined the Army at 17, and Rhonda was just a girl during the worst years. So that left Richard, wearing too-small hand-me-downs because Bob's paycheck rarely made it to the bank, waiting up on school nights to see whether his father would find his way home or need to be shouldered from the corner pub.

*

I wish I could remember the moments beyond the black, but maybe that veil is the mercy of the Universe, saying, *You shouldn't see yourself like this. You shouldn't know all the ways you've been seen.* There's a verse in Corinthians I've heard countless believers reference; it says a child of God will never be burdened with more temptation or tribulation than the Lord knows they can handle. And what is God but the Universe? Who am I but its child?

*

I hated being around Bob when he was drunk, Donna says of her father-in-law. *He was horrible to Betty* [his wife]*, but he would get all mushy with me.*

When she speaks about him she makes the same face she does when someone chews gum with their mouth open or says they like cilantro.

Donna's own mother, Mary Ann, was raised by abusive alcoholics, and when she was 15, they signed for her to marry Dennis, a 23-year-old Navy submariner who, as he tells it, looked Mary's father dead in the eye and said, *I can take better care of her than you can.*

Mary was pregnant by 16 and had three children by her early 20s. Dennis was out to sea at least six months of every year, and when he was home, he was angry and impatient, violent. A drinker, sure, but it was the smoking Mary picked on; it was the black cherry pipe tobacco she threatened to leave him over. Donna loved her father for their early-morning fishing trips and for the nights they couldn't sleep and met in the kitchen to talk life, back before he was sure of all the answers to it.

He's a deacon now, of a small-town Baptist church in southwest Missouri. He's a cancer survivor who lives in overalls and leads a men's Bible study from his chair at the head of his dining room table. He worries for the soul of his granddaughter, Donna's only child, whose heart has been hardened against the Spirit by sex and booze and questions she thinks the Bible can't answer; the granddaughter who no longer closes her eyes when he prays to Heavenly Father before Sunday lunch.

*

Was it consent if I don't remember giving it, in the morning waking up next to a man I know I didn't want? Trying to recall whether or not he and I kissed before we fucked; scanning the floor, digging through his bathroom trashcan, feeling at my stomach and thighs for evidence of protection or pull-out precaution. But even if I do find what I'm looking for—a limp, stretched skin or slick crust in the hairs below my bellybutton—for the next two weeks every baby will scream louder in the coffee shop while I try to read; my boobs will be more tender than they usually are when it's just PMS; and I'll take a pregnancy test that reads negative the day before I stain another pair of underwear.

*

I pour coffee into a cup because I know how to pour coffee into a cup. Everything else feels foreign. The two-year woman is plating sheet cake as a couple more people trickle in—one, a fellow twenty-something, quiet and unassuming, wearing a Carhartt jacket and a long ponytail. He takes a seat at the empty corner of the table and politely declines a piece of cake.

Celiacs, he says.

The meeting is held at a small rehab clinic, in a room behind a particleboard door that feels, unmistakably, like church-basement Sunday school. Another man I'm not supposed to name arrives with a box of donuts, and again, the twenty-something says, *Can't*—says, *Celiacs*.

Three laminated posters in a row on the wall illustrate the effects of cocaine, alcohol, and marijuana on color-coded organs. Dog-eared, bookmarked, bound and blue-covered copies of *Alcoholics Anonymous*, Fourth Edition, have been pulled from purses and oversized jacket pockets and set on the foldout table like the Bibles I'd grown up with, grown out of.

A worn-out copy of the Good Book, tattered and falling apart at the seams, is usually owned by a man who is not, said one of a dozen pastors I don't remember from my childhood.

*

The Lake, at its deepest point, reaches 1,336 feet. But this Lake is not a lake; she's a body, hungry for wood and canvas, bone and last breath. She is a body, aged and ageless, and I wouldn't have to ask for her to take me in and down and through, into the void. She'd fill me with a thorough quickness, but I'd be different from all the ones who came before, who live lifeless in her belly, in her womb. I'd give her the most of me.

*

There was a special game I only played at Bob and Betty's, but it wasn't a game to me then—it was a test of faith; it was eternity. Underneath the stairs, I would write letters to God telling him how much I loved and trusted him and wanted his will for my life, and how desperately I also wanted a sign that he was listening. I would seal each letter in an envelope, place them one at a time on the shag-carpet landing and, running back underneath the stairs, pray with my eyes squeezed tight for God to disappear them, a sign of his omnipotence and a testament to my unshakable faith. People at church had spoken of miracles, and I wanted my own.

It wasn't on those same stairs because Richard didn't grow up in that house, but they're all I can imagine when I play out one of the only stories he has told me about his father's alcoholism. He was a teenager, and it was a night Bob found his own way home from the pub. From the top of the stairs, Richard watched his father feel his way around in the dark, but when Bob got to the bottom of the stairs, he stumbled. His face hit the banister, and when he stood back up, one of his eyes had been forced out of its socket. Richard says his father took the eye in his hand and simply pushed it back into place before lying down on the couch.

*

After checking that I'm the only car on this stretch of street, I scream behind the wheel, with the windows rolled up and the radio at max volume. It isn't easy to find a place to scream—somewhere beyond the sphere of students and colleagues and administrators; somewhere far enough away from apartment neighbors, fellow hikers, and late-night Lake Superior skinny dippers. When I do it, I shake for the tension and release, and the blood in my ears turns a heavy heat. But sure as its snap and burst into existence, sure as the residual rasp in my throat, is the silence that follows the scream—a beautiful, instinctual pause; the mind and body waiting for whatever comes after something so primal, because nothing screams just because it can.

*

Hi, my name is Brenna, and I'm an alcoholic.
Hi, Brenna.
My head hurts, all the time.
(Nodding) (Knowing)
Withdrawal. You can't get away with treating your body like shit for so many years and escape the consequences. Trust me; we know.

(Nodding) (Knowing)
Hard candy. Your body misses the sugar. Hard candy.

*

When I'm drunk I don't remember the ingrown, overgrown, sticky, scabbed, swollen folds and hairs and pits of my body; I forget its foulness. When I'm drunk I'll fuck with the lights on, I'll ride on top because I've forgotten to worry the rhythm of hips; the outward curve of my stomach; the never-hard nipples capping a pair of soft, sagging breasts. When I'm drunk I am sex, and I am God, and I am every thought the world has never had.

*

Q: How do you keep a Baptist from drinking?
A: You stick him in a room with another Baptist.

*

Richard joined the military, too—the Air Force—when he was 19. Years later, his older brother Roger was dishonorably discharged for being drunk on duty, but Richard rose through the ranks. Both on remote tours in South Korea, he and Donna met, drunk, at the base bar and were married two months later, honeymooning in Seoul. Donna eventually sobered up for Jesus, and Richard sobered up for her. And then they made a child, just one, who required half of everything, blood and bone, and then halves of those halves, and so on, and it became a grab bag of histories until she resembled something whole.

*

I already know the Serenity Prayer when I attend my first meeting, but I can't recall how I learned it. Maybe it was one of the things Bob taught me on our walks to the corner store, like how to toss sidewalk maple seeds just to watch them fall. I never knew him as a drunk.

At the end of the meeting, everyone holds hands and says the Lord's Prayer. The first time I join in, I'm wary of the calm, easy surge of cadence and verse from my sober mouth, of a prayer I don't want that's been holding itself together inside of me. But the familiarity is a respite, and I bow my head in gratitude for something else as effortless as coffee in a Styrofoam cup.

*

My dog tries to drag me into the liquor store when we pass by on our walk because she knows where the sausages are, to the right of the register, and that the cashier will give her a biscuit while he rings up my gin or whiskey with tonic or bitters; ice and the pint of Ben & Jerry's I won't remember having eaten when I wake up tomorrow.

I say to her, *Sorry, not this time*, and a man on his way inside hears me and laughs, like he knows something I don't.

*

One of the men I'm not supposed to name says to me that at his first AA meeting, decades ago, he'd only ever been so nervous once before in his life—his first day on the job at the power plant as a young man, fresh out of college. He says he looked up at the ceiling covered in pipes and wires of someone else's design, a system it was now his job to map and memorize, veins running wild through a body he was meant to keep alive.

It took time, but before long, if you showed me a pipe or a wire, I could tell you exactly where to stick it. He laughs and then coughs. *Keep coming.*

*

Every day, at the same time, hundreds of herring and ring-billed gulls congregate on a graffitied rock just off the Lakeshore. They scream and they scream and they don't stop screaming, until they do.

Thanks to the editors & staff at the following publications for putting some of these pieces, in their various forms, out into the world:

"Nesting" in *Pleiades*
"The Cart or The Egg" in *Quarterly West*
"Two Weeks, Guaranteed" in *Storm Cellar*
"Patsy Sings for Me" in *Midwestern Gothic*
"What's Mine is Yours" in *Bayou Magazine*
"Anatomy of a Father, of a Moose" in *Fugue*
"All-Containered" in *Carve Magazine*
"Language" in *Maudlin House*
"tenure," "Slow Burn," and "Company" in *The Rumpus*
"Paperweight" in *Public Pool*
"Back to My Place" in *New Delta Review*
"grandad" in *The Dr. T. J. Eckleburg Review*
"Wüsthof Silverpoint II 10-Piece Set" in *Grist*
"Pet Euthanasia Consent" in *The Pinch*
"Motherlode" in *Booth*
"Forever Blonde" in *Hippocampus Magazine*
"Cukes" in *decomP*
"Sate" in *The Normal School*
"Twenty-Something" in *DIALOGIST*
"Hypochondria, or The Disease" in *DIAGRAM*
"Empire Blue" in *New South*
"-cosms" in *3:AM Magazine*
"We Are Not Saints" in *Indiana Review*

BRENNA WOMER is a prose writer, poet, and editor in flux. She teaches creative writing at Western Colorado University in Gunnison, where she lives with her partner and pit bull. She holds an MA in English from Missouri State University, an MFA in Creative Writing from Northern Michigan University, and is the author of the cross-genre chapbook *Atypical Cells of Undetermined Significance* (C&R Press, 2018). Her work has appeared in *The Normal School*, *Indiana Review*, *DIAGRAM*, *The Rumpus*, and elsewhere. For more, visit brennawomer.com.

CPSIA information can be obtained
at www.ICGtesting.com
Printed in the USA
LVHW111800200122
708968LV00005B/159